MONTANA JUSTICE

Please return on or before the latest date above.
You can renew online at *www.kent.gov.uk/libs*
or by telephone 08458 247 200

_____

_____

CHARTER MARK
CUSTOMER SERVICE EXCELLENCE

Libraries & Archives

Kent
County
Council

00884\DTP\RN\07.07   LIB 7

MONTANA JUSTICE

by

Floyd Rogers

Dales Large Print Books
Long Preston, North Yorkshire,
BD23 4ND, England.

British Library Cataloguing in Publication Data.

Rogers, Floyd
   Montana justice.

   A catalogue record of this book is
   available from the British Library

   ISBN   978-1-84262-638-2 pbk

First published in Great Britain in 1973 by Robert Hale Limited

Copyright © Floyd Rogers 1973

Cover illustration © Gordon Crabb by arrangement with
Alison Eldred

The moral right of the author has been asserted

Published in Large Print 2008 by arrangement with
Mr W. D. Spence

Dales Large Print is an imprint of Library Magna Books Ltd.

Printed and bound in Great Britain by
T.J. (International) Ltd., Cornwall, PL28 8RW

ONE

Matt Clements sat in his favourite armchair at the foot of the veranda steps where it had been brought for him for this special occasion. Behind him, on the veranda, the piano, fiddle and concertina played their waltz to which the dancers, on the grass in front of the long, low, ranchhouse, whirled beneath the darkening Montana sky.

Matt smiled contentedly, wrinkling even further his lined face, weather-worn by the outdoor life of a rancher. It was good to have so many people around him, friends and neighbours; friendships which had grown during the last twelve years since he had come here in 1874.

Long, colourful gingham frocks swirled as the ladies danced gracefully, in the arms of their husbands, sweethearts or friends, smartly dressed in tight trousers and frock-coats, with string-ties neatly tied at the collars of their fancy shirts. Everyone wore their best clothes and everyone had come to enjoy themselves and so reflect the pleasure they felt at the marriage which had taken place.

A flash of pride came into Matt's eyes as he watched his twenty-three year old daughter, Abigail, swing in time to the music, in the arms of husband, Frank Hollis. Bride of but a few hours, she looked radiantly happy and they were lost in a world of their own. As he looked at her, Matt's mind took him back to his own wedding day. 'Betty,' he whispered to himself and his eyes dampened. Abigail was so like her mother, without being as frail – she had her father's strength. Her long, black silk-like hair was parted in the middle and, tonight, swept down to her shoulders, framing her soft-featured, oval face. Her dark eyes flashed with happiness and a joy of the occasion, especially when she sensed an admiration for her dress, which she had made herself. Drawn tight at the waist it swept away in an almost excessive fullness. The top came to a round collar high on the neck and the sleeves ballooned to a tightness round the wrists. Its design was enhanced by the pattern of roses on a pink background.

Frank held his bride in his powerful arms and guided her in the dance with his strong but gentle hands. An outdoor life had tanned his rugged, handsome features. His brown eyes were alert, missing little around him but tonight they only had sight for Abigail, who had approved his white fancy shirt at the neck of which was bowed a black, thin tie. On top he wore a black frock-coat, and the matching trousers came over the tops of his black calf-length boots.

The music kept up its rhythm, and one by one the other couples moved to the edge of the square, formed by the poles from which hung the oil lamps, until only Abigail and Frank were dancing. On and on they danced unaware of what had happened, unaware that now they were the centre of everyone's admiration, unaware that now only the music broke the stillness of the Montana evening. One final whirl came with the last note and as they stopped, the spell between them was broken. They raised their hands to clap, and only then, when they glanced round, were they aware that they were the only couple in the dancing area. Their surprise changed to laughter, as the guests began to clap, and infectiously swept the crowd with it. Friends surged forward to admire and congratulate.

The leader of the three-man band announced, a quadrille, and, as people sorted themselves out, Abigail and Frank strolled hand in hand towards her father.

'They make a fine couple, Matt.'

Matt glanced up to see Bob Scammon and his wife Nancy, his friends and neighbours from the Hash Knife ranch, beside him.

'Sure do, Bob,' he agreed.

'And I'm mighty glad to see them married,' added Bob. 'Thought at one time Abigail might choose Carl Petersen. He had a lot to offer, plenty of money and the Flying Diamond, biggest ranch around here. Would have dazzled many a girl.'

'Aye,' agreed Matt but any further comment was cut short as Abigail and Frank joined them.

'All right, dad?' asked Abbe. 'Can we get you anything to eat?'

'No thanks,' said Matt.

'A drink?' asked Frank.

'Later,' replied Matt. 'I'm enjoying my friends at the moment.'

Abigail smiled at Nancy. 'I must say it again, Nancy. I do like that dress, and black suits you.'

'I wanted her to wear something brighter,' commented Bob.

'There are only a few women who can wear black without it having sombre effect, but Nancy's one of them,' put in Matt. 'I'd offer to dance with her if these legs would do it.'

Nancy inclined her head gracefully, acknowledging Matt's remarks which delighted her, for she had taken a lot of care over the making of this dress and had been extremely careful that she had exactly the right amount of white trimmings on the black, patterned silk, so that they did not detract from the contrast between the black and her fair-hair, bunched this evening, in the nape of her neck. It couldn't be said that she was pretty, her mouth was a little too big, though the lips were perfectly shaped, and her eyes, arched by thin eyebrows were a little wide set, but there was an attractiveness about Nancy which this dress accentuated and which made men look twice.

Bob smiled warmly, proud of his wife. The band struck up. Bob took his wife's hand, made their excuses and started to move away.

Suddenly the music was drowned by the crack of a rifle from the darkness of the trees which swept past the east side of the building towards the river.

In almost the same instant there was a startled scream, and shocked guests saw Frank Hollis stagger, collapse against the veranda steps and roll down to lie still at Abbe's feet.

Abigail's face paled as she stared with horror and disbelief at the still form of her husband, then silent sobs began to rack her body and she sank slowly to the ground.

The stillness seemed to last an eternity, but as Abigail's legs began to buckle Bob Scammon was at her side, grasping her in his strong arms, supporting her before she collapsed over the body of her husband, gently easing her back on the steps.

Soon pandemonium broke out. Guests shouted, some raced forward to the veranda steps, others, led by Sheriff Bill Matthews, ran for the trees in the direction of the shot, not caring that they were not armed.

'Who was it?'

'Where's the doc?'

'Sheriff, over here!'

'Came from the trees.'

Questions and suggestions came thick and fast.

Bob glanced up as someone dropped to the steps beside him. He saw his wife's pale, taut face from which her pale blue eyes stared with shock, asking the unanswerable questions. Who did it? and why?

'Hold her, Nan,' said Bob. Two strides took

him beside his old friend Matt, who was struggling to push himself out of his chair, battling against the grip of his crippling arthritis, wanting to get to his daughter's side to be of some help in her moment of anguish. 'Steady, Matt,' Bob placed firm hands on Matt's shoulders and eased him back on the chair. 'We'll do all we can.'

'But, Bob, Bob, why? What is it all about?' Matt looked up at Bob, his face twisted in anguish, wanting some explanation for this tragic happening in the midst of gaiety.

How Bob wished he could give an answer and relieve his friend's feelings. But he couldn't; the whole thing seemed senseless. As far as he knew Frank hadn't an enemy in the world.

One of the first to reach the veranda steps had been Carl Petersen and now he was on his knees beside Frank. The face was white and still but then Carl detected a slight breath. He looked up at Abbe.

'He's alive,' he whispered and then, realising his words made no impact, he spoke again loudly and sharply to penetrate the bewildered brain. 'Abbe! He's alive!' Cal turned his head. 'Doc!' he yelled over his shoulder. 'Doc Evans. He's alive.'

The crowd which had gathered round,

parted as a short, stocky, middle-aged man pushed his way through with, 'Let me in, let me past.'

The doctor dropped on his knees and examined Frank quickly. Carl was right, Frank was still alive.

Carl's words hadn't any effect on Abigail, but Nancy, relieved at the news, kept repeating them to her. Slowly Abigail turned her head and stared at Nancy almost unbelievingly. Then she turned with such suddenness that she was out of Nancy's arms before she could stop her. Abigail flung herself on her knees beside her husband.

'Frank! Frank!' She looked up wildly at the doctor. 'He's alive. Will he be all right?'

The doctor looked hard at her. 'We'll do our best Abbe, we'll do our best.' He looked beyond Abigail to Nancy, who had come forward behind her friend, and nodded. Then he turned to Carl and Bob. 'We must get him inside and as gently as you can.'

Bob nodded and called to his son. 'Hank, look after Mr Clements.'

'Sure Pa.' The well-built twenty-year-old came beside Matt's chair.

Nancy placed firm but gentle hands on Abigail's arms, helped her up, and moved her to one side as Bob and Carl, with other willing helpers stepped forward to take Frank in their strong hands.

Abigail watched, feeling utterly helpless as the little group moved past her up the steps. Nancy turned her and they followed slowly. It was only when the men carrying Frank reached the doorway that the mantle of helplessness dropped from Abigail. Suddenly the unreality of the ghastly happening vanished and she found herself aware of everything, with a shocked coldness replacing the helpless disbelief.

She tried to hurry forward but Nancy restrained her.

'It's all right, Nancy, it's all right. I must get things ready.'

Nancy realised it was no good trying to stop Abigail, that it would be better for her to be active now that the initial shock had vanished.

The two friends hurried into the house, but as they reached the steps Abigail stopped.

'Dad, how's Dad?' she asked, looking anxiously at Nancy.

'He's all right,' comforted Nancy. 'Hank and some of the others are bringing him in.'

Relief showed on Abigail's face and they hurried upstairs. They turned back the bedclothes and Frank was lowered gently on to them. The men moved back, allowing the doctor and Abigail close to the bed.

'Abbe, plenty of hot water.' He handed her some instruments. 'Boil those. Bob, Carl, I'd like you here. Everybody else out. Nancy stand by the door, let no one in, and I might need you.' The doctor issued his orders quickly and precisely and in a moment the room was clear.

'Bob, we'll have to get his coat off but we must be gentle.'

Bob nodded and eased Frank up in his strong arms so that the doctor and Carl were able to slip the coat off without too much trouble.

'Lie him on his face.'

Bob turned Frank over and the doctor went to work swiftly and carefully. He slit the shirt up the back to reveal the wound. The bullet had penetrated the small of the back but fortunately the distance of the shot had reduced some of the impact and it had not gone deep.

'Tell Nancy to hurry Abigail with the instruments and water.'

When Bob came back to the bedside the doctor was examining Frank.

'I'll have to get that bullet out,' he said. 'Carl, you hold his feet, Bob his arms. I want him as still as possible.'

Bob and Carl took up their positions and a moment later Abigail and Nancy hurried in with bowls of steaming water.

'Thank you,' said the doctor, as they placed them on the table. 'Abbe, I think you'd better wait outside.'

Abigail took one long look at her husband.

'Will he be all right?' There was deep concern in her voice and on her face when she looked at the doctor.

'I'll do my best, Abbe,' he said gently, leading her to the door. 'I'll let you know as soon as I can. Get some sheets and tear them up for bandages.'

When he had closed the door Doc Evans hurried back to the bed. 'Nancy, I'd like you to stay to help me but if you'd rather not—'

'No, Doctor, I'll do all I can to help you save Frank.'

The doctor nodded. He glanced at Bob and Carl indicating that they should take hold of Frank's limbs. With a precise incision he made a cut across the wound. Carefully holding back the skin and flesh he started to probe with the forceps, working quickly but carefully. He probed deeper, examining the damage done by the bullet with the utmost care.

It seemed an eternity to Nancy, Bob and Carl. Was he never going to find the bullet? Then suddenly they sensed an easing of the tension and the doctor straightened, carefully withdrew the forceps with which he held the bullet.

He dropped it on the table beside the bed. 'Swabs,' he said sharply, Nancy, holding the cotton swab in a pair of tweezers, dipped it into the bowl of water and held it out for the doctor, who said no more as he took swab after swab from Nancy and carefully bathed the wound.

When he was satisfied he said, 'Thanks, Nancy, get the sheets from Abbe.' He glanced at Bob and Carl. 'It's all right now, you can let go. I'll want him easing up so I can bandage him.'

Nancy returned with the sheets torn in strips and, while Bob held Frank round the stomach raising him so that he could be bandaged, she helped the doctor.

A low moan came from Frank. The movement had stirred him into consciousness. Nancy looked at him anxiously and Carl moved to him in case he was needed, but Frank showed no sign of recognition.

He felt as if he was crawling out of a deep, dark canyon after a heavy fall. Somehow he must struggle to the top, to the light, which for a few moments didn't get any nearer. It was taking all his strength to drag his body along for his legs seemed useless; there was no power in them, in fact he wondered if they were there at all. Then suddenly the light seemed to rush at him. Something was gripping his stomach and there was a tightness all about him. He couldn't move his legs. A panic seized him but he couldn't do anything about it; he seemed fixed in helplessness.

'Right, I've finished, lower him gently.' The voice was vague and distant but he felt an easing around his stomach and then the softness of the bedclothes.

Where was he? What had happened? He tried to turn his head. 'Easy, Frank, take it easy.' The voice was nearer. Then he heard footsteps.

The doctor crossed the room to the door. 'You can come in now, Abigail,' he said quietly when he looked outside. 'Frank is beginning to come round.'

Abbe came into the room. 'Will he be all right?' she asked anxiously.

'There is every chance that he should be but it's too soon to say. The bullet didn't get to the spinal cord, if it had he'd have been paralysed. He's lost a lot of blood and sustained a heavy shock. He'll need careful nursing for a time. Now go to him.'

Abbe hurried to Frank and dropped on her knees beside him. There was no recognition. She looked anxiously at the doctor who came forward and gave Frank a brief examination.

'It's all right, Abbe. He's just lost consciousness again.'

Nancy glanced at Bob who, reading her thoughts nodded. 'I'll stay with you tonight, Abbe,' she said. 'You should get some sleep.'

'I'll be all right,' replied Abbe. 'There's no need for you to stay.'

'I think it's a good idea,' put in Doctor Evans. 'I'll stay for a while but you want someone around after I've gone.'

Abbe started to protest again. She wanted to be alone with Frank when he regained consciousness. The doctor put a stop to her protestations. 'You'll be needed tomorrow and the next day and for lots more days, Abbe, tonight it would be better to let Nancy stay here.'

'I'll be only too glad to, Abbe,' reassured Nancy.

Abbe nodded weakly. 'Thank you.'

'Now we'll go and see your father, he'll be

anxious,' said the doctor.

'And I'll see if the sheriff has found anything,' said Bob. 'Coming Carl?'

The four of them left the bedroom and Nancy settled down on a chair beside the bed.

After Abigail and the doctor had relieved Matt's anxiety he was persuaded to go to bed. Bob and Carl hurried from the house, reassuring guests who had waited for news that Frank had every chance of pulling through.

The guests were shattered by the tragedy. Everyone wanted to help, to do something to alleviate the hurt which was now searing through a household loved and respected in this part of Montana. But there was little anyone could do except hope and pray.

There was an outbreak of shouting amongst the pines and Bob broke away from one group of enquirers to hurry in that direction. He arrived upon a group of men who had just been joined by the sheriff.

'What is it?' asked Bob.

'Found the spot from which the shot was fired,' replied the sheriff, 'but I'm afraid it doesn't help very much. It's too dark to follow any possible trail now, but I'll give it a try in the morning.'

21

'Doubt if you'll come up with much,' observed Bob, 'whoever it was would have his get-a-way carefully planned and I suspect he'd use the river, it's fairly shallow here-abouts.'

'If he did then the task will be hopeless,' said Bill Mathews, 'but I'll scout around in daylight.' He turned to the men who had been helping. 'Thanks, boys, I'd appreciate some help in the morning, if any of you can spare the time.'

'Sure,' the men answered as one, all eager to bring the gunman to justice. They wanted revenge on the man who could shoot down the likeable Frank Hollis in cold blood.

The group started to break up and Bob and the sheriff walked to the house together.

'This is a puzzling one, Bob,' said Bill. 'Who'd want to kill Frank? He's a popular man, I've never known him cross anyone, and to do it tonight of all nights.'

'I've been racking my brain to find an answer, but can't,' said Bob. 'It's got me beat.'

'Do you think Abigail will be up to answering a few questions?' asked the sheriff.

'I reckon so; she went to pieces at first but soon got a grip on herself. Shouldn't make it too long.'

'I won't; but I wondered if she could tell

us anything about Frank's past; might be a connection there.'

'Mm,' Bob was thoughtful, 'could be, but I can't help you. All I know is he rode in here seven years ago, Matt gave him a job, liked what he saw. You know Matt, he'd use his own judgement and ask no questions.'

When they reached the house, guests were beginning to disperse; there was nothing more anyone could do. As they stepped on to the veranda Carl Petersen came out of the house.

'Any luck?' he asked.

'No,' replied the sheriff. 'I'll try to pick up a trail in the morning.' He stepped past Carl into the house. Bob was following him when Carl stopped him.

'I've told Abbe to let me know if there's anything I can do. I know you'll be around, Bob, but don't forget if I can help I'll…'

'Thanks, Carl,' cut in Bob. 'I don't suppose there will be anything but if there is – thanks. It'll be a question of how Frank gets on.'

They bade each other goodnight and Bob went inside. The sheriff was talking to Abbe. She was shaking her head and Bob judged that she knew no more about Frank's past than he did.

Suddenly Hank appeared at the top of the stairs. 'Pa!' he called out, 'get up here quick, Mister Clements is giving a bit of trouble.'

At the sound of his voice the people in the hall turned and looked up but Bob was the first to the stairs. Abigail left the sheriff without another word and was close behind Bob. When they reached the bedroom they saw Matt trying to get out of bed.

'Get me up, get me up,' he called. 'I want to see that coyote Petersen.'

Bob and Hank gripped Matt firmly but gently and eased him back into bed in spite of his struggling. Abigail was beside him. 'Dad, please take it easy. Things are bad enough.'

'Petersen did it! Petersen did it!' shouted Matt.

'Quiet, Matt,' urged Bob. 'Simmer down.'

'He did! I know he did!'

'Dad. Don't say such foolish things,' said Abigail. 'Carl was at the party so how could he?'

'A man don't have to fire the shot to be behind it,' yelled Matt. 'Get me to him. I'll soon get it out of him.'

Bob glanced at Hank and formed the word Doc with his lips. Hank hurried from the room to return a few moments later with Doc Evans.

'Matt! Settle down.' His voice was firm and sharp.

'Nonsense, Doc. I won't settle down until I've seen…'

'You won't see anybody the way you're going on,' cut in the doctor. 'Think of Abbe, she has enough trouble without you going on like this. Simmer down and we'll see what we can do for you in the morning.' The doctor pressed him firmly back on the pillow.

Matt knew it was useless to fight against Doc Evans so he succumbed reluctantly, muttering under his breath. Besides the doc was right about Abbe. The old man turned to his daughter. 'I'm sorry for being a nuisance.'

'That's all right, Dad,' Abigail bent down and kissed him. 'Just settle down now; we'll talk in the morning.'

Bob was the last to leave the bedroom and as he reached the door Matt called him back. 'Bob, come and talk to me tomorrow; I'm right.'

'Sure, I'll see you in the morning, Matt. Now settle down and don't worry Abbe. Nancy's going to sit with Frank so's Abbe can get some sleep, and I'll be around.'

'Thanks,' said Matt.

Matt knew he could rely on Bob to be there in the morning to listen to him. It was good to have two such friends as Bob and Nancy Scammon and he knew they would take good care of Abbe tonight.

Matt had always marvelled that the age gap between fifty-six and thirty had made no difference to the happiness of their marriage. Everyone in Lewistown and the neighbouring ranches had been surprised three years ago when Bob Scammon returned from a fortnight in Great Falls, the nearest town of any considerable size two hundred miles away, with a bride twenty-six years younger than himself.

There were those who cast their doubts about the marriage working out, the difference between the ages was too much; Bob wouldn't be able to hold her in a quiet place like the Hash Knife; a woman in the prime of life, among young ranch hands would not make things easier for the older Bob, and there was Bob's son, Hank, at eighteen how would he take to a new mother of twenty-seven? Well, all the doubters had been proved wrong. Nancy had fitted into the ranch-life as if she had always been used to it, and the cowboys who rode for Bob liked and respected her; Nancy saw to it that no trouble blew up on her account, and Hank had been glad for his father's sake.

Bob thought the world of Nancy without offering any disrespect to his first wife, who had been tragically killed when her horse bolted with the buckboard she was driving back from town. Bob had grieved for four years, threw himself more and more into the work of the ranch and tried to build a different life. He seemed to have immersed himself in the life of a widower until he went to Great Falls, where he met and fell in love with Nancy who, much to his surprise, accepted the proposal from a man nearly twice as old as she.

Nancy had brought a new life to Bob and to the Hash Knife and everyone was pleased to see the marriage working out, most of all Matt Clements.

He was grateful to Nancy for the deep friendship and love of a woman which she had brought to Abigail, something which Abigail had never had. True, she had friends in town, and she could count many as such, but as her mother had died soon after Abigail was born she had missed that deep feminine affection.

Matt had done a good job of bringing up his daughter and, in spite of it being in a man's world of ranching, Abigail had kept that femininity inherited from the kind and gentle mother she had never known. Matt had often wished for his wife's help in bringing up their daughter, and many folks said that she needed a woman around, but Matt had never shown the inclination to marry again.

From Nancy's first visit to the Rocking Chair she and Abigail had taken to each other in spite of the seven years difference in their ages; Nancy seemed to have a gift for spanning the age gap. Matt knew she would give all the comfort and help that Abigail needed tonight.

Bob left the room his mind full of the outburst. When he got downstairs everyone had gone except the doctor and the sheriff who stood talking close to the front door, and Hank who was waiting at the bottom of the stairs.

'Nancy and I are staying here tonight,' he explained, 'you can go on home.'

'Right, Pa.' He turned to go but Bob stopped him. 'Not a word of Matt's outburst to anyone.'

Hank looked anxiously at his father. 'You think there might be something in it?'

Bob pursed his lips. 'Doubt it, but who

knows. Best not to spread those sort of theories around though.'

'I'll just take another look at Frank,' said Doctor Evans, 'then I'll ride back into town with Bill.'

Bob nodded and walked up the stairs with the doctor. They found Abigail and Nancy beside the bed. Frank, pale against the sheets, was resting peacefully.

'Has he come round again?' asked the doctor.

'No,' replied Nancy.

The doctor examined Frank, gave a satisfactory grunt and turned to the anxious Abigail. 'He's just the same and the longer he sleeps the better for him. There's nothing more you can do so get some sleep. I'll be here first thing in the morning.'

Abigail saw the doctor and the sheriff out of the house and returned to the room in which her husband lay. She stayed a short while, then fixed Bob up in another bedroom and she too went to bed after getting Nancy to promise to wake her when Frank showed any sign of recovery.

It was a tired and worried Abigail who flopped into a bed which she should have been sharing with her husband on their honeymoon.

Sleep was not easy to come by. The sight of Frank staggering, falling against the steps and rolling down to her feet, kept coming to her, and again and again she heard the shot which had shattered the happy evening and left her in a lonely bed. Who could have done it? Why try to kill Frank? What was behind this apparently senseless shooting? Question after question tumbled across her brain but she could not answer them. Her father's accusation flung itself at her time and time again but she dismissed it as utter nonsense. Carl wanted to marry her but he was not a jealous man who would resort to killing to get her.

Abigail dozed fitfully and was wide awake immediately the door opened about midnight. She reached out and turned up the oil lamp to find Nancy approaching the bed.

'Abbe, Frank seems to be coming round.'

Abigail jumped out of bed, grabbed a cloak and was out of the door almost before Nancy realised it. They ran into Frank's room where he was stirring in half consciousness.

He moaned deeply as if in pain, and his head twisted from side to side. Gradually he stopped and his breathing became steadier. His eyes flicked open only to close as quickly again. Abigail said nothing but just stood there holding her husband's cold hand. Nancy watched anxiously from the other side of the bed.

Gradually the flickering stopped and Frank stared unseeingly into the room.

'Frank, Frank, it's me, Abbe,' she whispered softly. Frank showed no sign that he had heard. Abigail glanced anxiously at Nancy and then tried again. This time there was a slight turning of Frank's head in the direction of the sound.

Nothing made sense to him, there was only a blur but a faint noise attracted his attention. There it was again; the same sound. Slowly before his eyes a figure began to appear. It had little shape but it stood out against the background. His head throbbed. He tried to move to ease his head but he couldn't. It seemed to be held in a vice-like grip. He attempted to move his legs but he couldn't. Then he remembered trying to do it before. His brain pounded. He couldn't move, he must be paralysed. Paralysed! The word beat in his mind. His body felt so numb.

'Frank, Frank, it's me, Abbe.' 'Paralysed' receded, driven back by the gentle sound, but it remained there. Slowly the form started to take shape.

'Can you hear me, Frank, it's Abbe.'

Abbe! The word suddenly burst in his brain. His vision cleared and Abigail stood before him sharp and beautiful.

'Abbe,' Frank's dry lips formed the word which came as a whisper between them.

Abigail's brain pounded with relief. Frank recognised her. Tears started to flow and Abigail dropped to her knees and buried her head close to Frank's.

'Oh! Frank, Frank, I love you,' she sobbed.

She did not move until she had cried the relief out of herself. Then she pushed herself from the pillow.

'What happened? Where am I?' asked Frank as Abigail straightened herself.

'Do you remember the party?' The voice came from his left.

Frank turned his head slowly and saw someone else standing close to the bed. 'Nancy,' he whispered.

Abigail and Nancy exchanged glances, and there was a heart-felt relief in their eyes. Frank knew them.

'Party?' Frank went on. 'My wedding...' He turned back to Abbe, a look of horror in his eyes. 'Abbe! Our wedding. There was a shot. Me!'

Abigail nodded. 'Yes, but you're going to be all right.'

Again Frank was aware of the numbness in his body. There was a restricting tightness.

'Abbe, Abbe! What's happened to me?' There was a panic in his voice. Alarm showed on his face, and he made an effort to move.

'Frank, you must lie still,' urged Nancy, pressing his shoulders back. 'You've been badly wounded and must keep still.'

Keep still. The words seemed to thunder into Frank's mind and a single word pounded into their place. Paralysed.

He stared wide eyed at Abbe. 'Paralysed, I'm paralysed,' he whispered incredulously.

'No! No!' answered Abbe. The urgent note in her voice failed to make an impression.

'I am! I am! My body's numb, I can't move my legs.' There was panic in Frank's voice and sweat rolled from his forehead.

Abigail and Nancy looked at each other; alarm showed in their faces.

'I'll get Bob,' said Nancy and hurried from the room.

Abigail was still trying to reassure Frank who was struggling to move his legs, when Bob and Nancy came into the room. Four strides took Bob to the bedside. He grasped

Frank by the shoulders forcing him back on the pillow.

'Lie still, Frank, you'll open the wound if you don't,' he ordered brusquely.

'I'll never move again if I don't now,' snapped Frank wildly.

'Nonsense,' rapped Bob, 'you'll do more damage if you try to move.'

'That's what you say.'

'It's true.'

'I'm paralysed!'

'Rubbish, lie still.'

'Frank, please try and be reasonable,' put in Abigail anxiously. 'You'll be all right if you are careful and take things quietly as the doctor said. Please do as he says.'

Frank sank back against the pillows, exhausted with the struggle. He couldn't make them understand. 'All right,' he muttered, resigned to the inevitable. He closed his eyes and the three friends stayed with him until he was asleep again.

Abigail looked anxiously at him, worried that what he said was true. The doctor could be wrong, maybe the bullet had caught the spinal cord. Nancy came to her.

'Come on, Abbe, we'll make some coffee. Bob will stay with Frank.' Reluctantly Abbe turned from the bed and walked to the door; she knew it was no good staying. Sleep was the best thing for Frank.

The following morning Doc Evans was out at the Rocking Chair by eight o'clock. Abigail and Bob quickly related what had happened during the night. The doctor frowned. He didn't like the sound of it but did not betray his fears to Abigail.

'He's going to be all right, Abbe, so don't worry. This is probably only a natural reaction on regaining consciousness. Let's hope he's forgotten all about it this morning.'

They went up to the bedroom to find Nancy wiping Frank's face with a damp cloth.

'Hello, Frank, how are you this morning?' asked the doctor brightly as he crossed to the bed.

Frank, who had been lying quietly, was roused when he saw the doctor.

'Doc, Doc, you tell them I'm right. I'm paralysed aren't I?'

'Of course you're not,' replied the doctor.

Frank stared at him. 'Come on, Doc, don't give me that talk. I can't move my legs.'

'Sure you can,' said Doc Evans. 'But you've got to be careful. That's a nasty wound you've got in your back but it'll mend and you'll be as good as the next man.'

'Doc, I can't move my legs,' repeated Frank firmly.

'Let me have a look,' Doc Evans turned the bed clothes back and examined Frank's legs. 'They're all right,' he said, 'you can move them.'

Frank tried with no success. 'There, there I told you I can't,' he cried, 'I'm paralysed.'

'Nonsense Frank.' The doctor could still see the doubt in Frank's eyes. 'You're going to be all right, but you must be careful of that wound, you must let it heal.'

'In other words, lie still – I'm paralysed.'

'I didn't say that.'

Frank was exhausted by his excitement and, with a deep sigh, sank back against the pillow. It was useless, no one would believe him.

A few moments later Doc Evans was outside the room with Abigail, reassuring her of Frank's welfare.

'He'll be all right, Abbe. His back will feel tender and numb and no doubt as this disappears so his obsession with paralysis will disappear. Nurse him carefully and keep trying to instil into him that he is not paralysed.'

Abbe returned to Frank, knelt beside his bed and kissed him.

Frank's arms closed round her and held her tightly.

'Abbe, this is a fine start to our marriage, an end as well. A pity that bullet didn't kill me.'

'Frank! You mustn't talk like that. I'm glad you're alive. You're NOT paralysed. You will walk again and be just as active as you were before.'

'I'm a helpless cripple and will be for the rest of my life.'

TWO

When Bob went to Matt's room after the doctor had gone Matt's first concern was for Abigail and Frank. After he had been reassured that his daughter was all right and that Frank was as well as could be expected under the circumstances but was in no danger, Matt turned to the subject of his outburst the previous night.

'Sit down, Bob,' he said indicting a chair. 'You know what I said yesterday, well I've had a long night to think about it and I'm more convinced than ever that Carl Petersen was behind the shooting.'

'But, Matt—' started Bob.

'Hear me out before you say anything,' interrupted Matt. 'You, yourself said that you thought at one time Abbe might marry Carl.'

'Yes. A lot of people thought that, after all Carl had a lot to offer apart from his dark, good-looks inherited from his mother's Spanish ancestors.'

'Right,' agreed Matt. 'He's a ladies man

but thank goodness Abigail saw beneath the surface and changed her mind.'

'I know he can be ruthless like his father.'

'Sure, but with a difference, Lee Petersen would fight in the open; Carl has a streak of meanness in him which would make him do anything to get what he wanted, especially if he felt he'd been done out of it. This side of him can be blamed on being a spoilt only child.'

Bob nodded. 'But he can be so charming and likeable; he was at the party last night; he helped when Frank was shot. I can't see him being the instigator of a cold-blooded killing.'

'That's just what blinds people to the other side of Carl Petersen. His niceties cover up the streak of mean ruthlessness in his complex character. I believe there's part of Carl Petersen that could and would kill if the prize was big enough. You know as well as I do that Carl Petersen dreams of a cattle empire, his Flying Diamond, my Rocking Chair and your Hash Knife all as one big ranch. He's made you offers, Bob.'

'Sure,' agreed Bob, 'but I won't sell.'

'Right. Now he's not made me an offer because he reckoned he'd get the Rocking Chair by marrying Abigail.'

Bob looked thoughtful. 'And if he did that he could force me to sell by cutting off most of my water supply by damaging the river where it branches on Rocking Chair land.'

Matt smiled. 'Now, you're catching on. Abbe's marriage to Frank wrecked all that.'

'But why wait until the wedding night to try to kill Frank.'

'Remember, Carl went east a month before the wedding, a business with pleasure trip, well, the wedding wasn't arranged until after he'd gone. He didn't know of the serious relationship between Abbe and Frank. He thought he'd be the one; you see Abbe had never told him that she wasn't serious about him, a mistake on her part, and when he had gone away she saw a chance to have everything settled by the time Carl returned.'

Bob nodded, he was beginning to see what Matt was getting at. 'Carl returned the day of the wedding to find the invitation had not been sent on to him; told me himself, he got a shock when he got back.'

'There was nothing he could do about it then as far as persuading Abbe to marry him went – he was too late. He saw the chance of a cattle empire disappearing. If he wanted it he had to do something drastic

40

like eliminating Frank, waiting his time and then proposing to Abigail.'

Bob grunted. 'It's an explanation, it's possible but I don't think Carl would go to that extent. Shooting Frank last night was a bit risky.'

'Nevertheless it happened. If the stakes were big enough, and I reckon Carl figured they were, then the risk was worth it. Thank goodness it didn't quite come off.'

'But Carl was so pleasant last night. There was nothing about him to suggest–'

'Of course not. His charm was a cover. Who would associate him with the shooting?'

'Surely later would have been a better time to try.'

'More risk of the person firing the shot being caught – last night there was bound to be confusion with so many people about.'

'Well, I don't know,' mused Bob. He was reluctant to accuse a man without proof.

'Well, I do,' snapped Matt. 'It's the only possible explanation; the only reason there can be for the shooting.'

Bob thought for a moment. 'What about someone out of Frank's past?'

'Nonsense.'

'But what do you know about it?'

'You know me, Bob, I take a man on what I see. When Frank rode in here I liked what I saw and asked no questions. Frank couldn't have done anybody any harm. Besides if that was the case why hadn't they shown up before. No, Bob, I reckon I'm right and I want you to put my ideas to the sheriff. He's probably out here by now.'

It was a thoughtful Bob Scammon who crossed to the window and looked out.

'Yes, there are some men amongst the trees towards the river, guess it'll be Bill Mathews and his deputies.'

'Then get out and tell them to stop wasting their time and get Carl Petersen.' Matt's voice rose with urgency.

'All right, Matt, quieten down. I'll see Bill.' He started towards the door then stopped and turned back to Matt. 'Can I give you a bit of advice, Matt? Don't voice these opinions to anyone else, certainly not to Abigail. She has enough worry at present and puts your outburst last night down to shock, tension and the upset. Leave it that way.'

Matt nodded. 'All right, Bob. Now get off and see Bill.'

Bob took the sheriff to one side when he found him examining the river bank for tracks. The sheriff was surprised by Matt's idea but had to agree that it was possible after hearing the full account. He walked back to the house with Bob and was soon confronting Matt.

'I'm not saying you're wrong and I'm not saying you're right, Matt,' he said. 'You've given me an idea so I want you to promise to leave it to me from here-on.' He grinned. 'I know you Matt, but I'm asking you not to say or do anything. Abbe and Frank don't want upsetting at a time like this and, most important, don't challenge Carl Petersen. He's sure to be coming here offering help but please don't say anything to make him suspicious. If you are right, it will take some proving and we may have to play a waiting game.'

Matt eventually saw that the sheriff made sense and he agreed to hold his tongue, something he found difficult to do in the ensuing days when Carl visited the ranch as a friendly neighbour, offering help and visiting Frank, especially as the sheriff got no further in his search for the would-be killer. He had vanished completely without a trace and if Carl Petersen was involved it certainly was going to be a waiting game.

Abigail hoped that she would never again

have to face a week like the one which followed the shooting. Every visit to Frank's room tore at her heart and mind saddened by the sight of a once active man lying helpless on the bed, convinced in his own mind that he would never walk again. The agony of those moments, the depths of despair to which she saw Frank sink, were almost too much for her but she knew that if she once gave way, if she weakened for one moment, all would be lost. She was the one thing Frank had to cling to and she knew that as long as she had the strength there was a chance that she would beat Frank's obsession.

The numbness and soreness eased in Frank's body but use did not return to his legs, as the doctor had hoped, and Frank became more and more certain that he would never walk again. Time and time again the scene was similarly repeated.

'You'd be better off if that bullet had killed me.'

'Frank! Don't talk like that!'

'Of course you would, Abbe. You'd have been free to marry a virile, active man instead of looking after a cripple.'

'Frank, it's you I love; it's you I married and it's you I want, no one else. You are my life and I can manage until you are up and about again.'

'Please don't fool yourself, Abbe, please don't live on false hopes. I'm crippled for life; I won't walk again. If I was going to walk I'd be getting some use into my legs by now.'

'Frank I'm certain you will walk again.' Abbe put all the conviction she could into her voice trying to impress her husband that the situation was not hopeless. 'You must give it time but you must also be convinced yourself that you will, Doc Evans says you will.'

'Doc Evans isn't me; he may have a hope, but he doesn't really know what damage that bullet has done. I know my legs are useless, just as I'm useless to you.'

'You're not useless to me, if you had to lay here for the rest of your life, which you won't, I would still need you to help me run the ranch, I would need you to advise me and tell me what to do. That would take a lot of the burden off me, we'll have to appoint a foreman and then you could deal direct with him.' Abbe put all the enthusiasm into her voice trying to raise the interest in Frank, trying to give him something to occupy his mind to combat the depression.

Alone, Abbe weakened, she cried and it needed a great strength of will to face another day of trying to pull Frank back from the brink of utter despair. Abbe believed she would have succumbed to the strain if it had not been for the support of her father and her friends, especially Nancy and Bob Scammon. They were daily visitors, eager to do all they could to ease the strain Abigail was under. Bob organised the ranch work consulting Matt while Nancy was a pillar of strength to Abigail. Doc Evans came daily, satisfied with Frank's medical progress but a little worried that Frank's attitude showed no sign of changing.

Six days after the shooting Abbe had a particularly trying session with Frank, she could not impress upon him that there was every chance he would walk again and could not stir his interest in the ranch. Frank seemed to be at a new low and it tore at Abbe to see him this way. She sensed an antagonism to her efforts.

'But Frank it's the only way to run the ranch, we must–'

'Damn the ranch!' Frank suddenly burst out. 'It's not ours, Matt was handing over after our honeymoon, well we haven't had a honeymoon. You can tell him to forget about giving it to us. I'm useless; I'll never be able to run it, stop pestering me about running the ranch. I can't do it and you know it. You're just trying to humour me.' Tears began to fill in Abigail's eyes as Frank went on. He had been difficult, but he had never turned on her, never stormed or shouted at her. 'I'm tired of being told I'm going to be all right, tired of hearing what I can do. I can do nothing, I know I'm just a useless hulk, so forget trying to help me forget–' Suddenly Abbe burst into tears and, with sobs racking her body, she flung open the door and ran from the room.

The door to Matt's room was ajar. From his chair beside the window he heard the sobs and rush of feet along the corridor.

'Abbe! Abbe!' he shouted his voice carrying that authoritative note which demanded obedience. It was a tone he had very rarely had to use with anyone, and least of all with Abigail, but now he suddenly sensed his daughter needed him.

The footsteps turned to his room, the door flew open and Abbe flung herself on her knees beside her father burying her head against his chest. A loving, comforting arm enfolded her shoulder.

'What's the matter Abbe? Frank been a bit

trying?' The voice was soft and soothing. 'Cry it out and then tell me.'

Matt waited patiently until the sob-racked body quietened and the final tears ceased.

'Now do you feel like telling me about it?' he asked.

Abigail hesitated. Had she been too impetuous? Was she at fault? Had she really got on to Frank about the ranch too much?

'Well?' Matt asked again.

Abbe raised her head and through her bloodshot eyes saw the love and kindness she had seen whenever she had gone to her father with her girlish troubles. She saw understanding and wisdom in the ruggedness, and warmth in his smile and she realised that even though she was a married woman her father was still there to help if she wanted, but he would not interfere.

Abbe straightened herself and wiped her eyes with her handkerchief.

'I'm sorry, Dad.'

'Don't be sorry, a good cry does you good sometimes. Well, what went wrong, anything I can help you with?'

'Frank is more depressed than ever today. I can't persuade him that he may walk again, it's hopeless Dad, it's like trying to break through a wall. Maybe he's right, maybe Doc

Evans is wrong, maybe his spine was damaged.'

'Steady, lass. It's early days yet. Doc said it might take a while, but it's not just that which has upset you.'

'I thought I was getting Frank interested in the ranch, showing him that he's needed to run it but just now he said he wasn't interested, said I was pestering him about it, just trying to humour him. He doesn't want the ranch, Dad, he said so, said you've to keep it, he could never run it.'

'He's talking nonsense, Abbe. Of course he can run it. Come on, help me to my feet. I'll go to see him.'

'No, Dad, not in his present mood.'

'There's no time like now. Probably the best time to make him see sense.'

'Let me try again.'

'No, Abbe, failure again will upset you too much. Besides Frank might take it better from someone else. Don't look so worried, Abbe, I'll not interfere in anything which has gone between you two. I won't be able to make him see that there is a chance of walking again but I might be able to get him to take an interest in the ranch. Come on now, help me up.' Matt reached for his stick, putting an end to any further objections by Abigail.

With some painful effort, and with Abbe's help, Matt struggled to his feet and along the corridor. When they neared Frank's door Matt stopped.

'Go on, away with you, I'll manage from here,' he whispered.

Abbe hesitated, saw the determination on her father's face and then hurried quietly away. From the end of the corridor she watched Matt struggle towards Frank's room, saw him disappear and heard the door shut.

Matt saw Frank's face pale against the pillow. He looked gaunt; the shock, the forced inactivity and no fancy for food had taken their toll and Matt felt for the man who had once been his hard-working, no-nonsense foreman.

'Howdy, Frank,' Matt greeted as he shuffled towards the chair beside the bed.

Frank did not answer as he stared at the efforts of the older man who found relief when he sat down.

'How are you feeling today?'

Again Frank did not answer the question but said, 'I expect Abbe has told you what I said about the ranch.'

Matt nodded. 'Yes, but I aren't taking any

notice of it. The ranch will still be yours and Abbe's. The documents will all be ready in a week's time – the day you were due back from your honeymoon.'

'It's no good giving it to us now,' rapped Frank. 'I can't run it and it would be too much for Abbe.'

'And why can't you run it?' replied Matt.

'Why!' Frank's laugh was hollows. 'I would have thought that was pretty obvious.'

'Obvious? It's not. If you mean your legs–'

'That's exactly what I do mean,' cut in Frank roughly. 'How can I run a ranch as useless as I am.'

'You aren't useless!' snapped Matt. 'How do you think I managed?'

'Yours is different. It came on gradually and you can still get about.'

'Yes I can and nobody knows what it has cost me in pain and determination. I could have been helpless long ago if I had given way to it but I was determined to keep going. Oh! yes it hurt, deep down it hurt, especially when I realised I was no longer as active as I was, that no longer could I stand alongside any man and do as he did. Yes, it was a gradual slowing up, but you know how it's been this last couple of years. I could have said it was impossible for me to run the

Rocking Chair. I had a good foreman in you. You're still good. Just stop feeling sorry for yourself. I knew I couldn't get better, you don't; I knew I would get worse, you don't; you have a hope, I hadn't. Just get it into your head that there is a chance you will walk again but even if there isn't you can still run the ranch. Get a good foreman like I did.' There was no stopping Matt especially when he saw by the expression on Frank's face that his words were getting home. 'You've got one thing I didn't have when I slowed down – you've got a wife. If she isn't worth making the effort for I don't know what is. She firmly believes you'll get better, that the pair of you will run the ranch as two active people, and even if you can't then she's willing to do it but she needs you to give her the support and the strength. Not the other way round in this case, oh yes you'll need her for many things but to stay here, to run the ranch she'll need you. Make no mistake about it, Frank, you and Abbe are getting the ranch, what's happened to you makes no difference, I promised it would be your wedding present and I'm not going back on my word now.'

'But Matt, I can't–'

'No buts and no can'ts,' cut in Matt

roughly. 'You can and you will.'

'I'll need your help,' said Frank weakly.

'You won't and you're not getting it. You know me well enough, Frank. I'll not interfere in what's Abbe's and yours. Advice if you want it, help in the way you mean it, no! A week ago you thought you were capable of running this ranch, well, you still are. At least make the effort for Abbe's sake, she's near the end of her tether with worry, and seeing you as she saw you today only makes it worse. A week today the ranch will legally belong to you both but you can start running it right away, as from now I'm finished, so start making your plans, Frank.'

Matt pushed himself to his feet. He looked hard at Frank who said nothing. Matt could tell he was thinking hard on his words. The older man turned and shuffled towards the door. He grasped the knob.

'Thanks, Matt.' The voice was husky. Matt turned, smiled, nodded and went out.

Abbe had spent an anxious time wondering what was passing between her husband and her father, and when she heard the door of Frank's room close she hurried into the corridor. She felt some measure of relief when she saw the smile on Matt's face.

53

'Is he all right?' she queried anxiously.

'I think so, I hope so,' replied Matt. 'Hold it!' He halted Abbe as she turned towards the door. 'Help me back to my own room; it'll give him time to think before you go to him.'

Frank stared at the door as it closed behind Matt. It had taken the old man something of an effort to cross the room and it was only now that Frank realised what it must have cost Matt to visit him every day since the shooting. He had never really thought of how hard it must have been for Matt to continue running the ranch, and, now he thought about it he had to admit he had never once heard Matt complain or express a sorrow for himself. He frowned when he realised that this was just what he had been doing. His feelings for himself had blinded him to the feelings of others. Suddenly he felt small as he recalled the true stature of the crippled man who had just left him.

Abbe pushed the door open apprehensively but hopefully. Her heart missed a beat when she saw the frown on Frank's face, but relief came to her when she saw him raise his head, smile and hold out his hand to her. She rushed forward, took it and fell on her knees beside the bed. Tears filled her eyes.

'Abbe, I'm sorry,' said Frank gently. 'Sorry for what I said this morning and sorry for being such a rotten patient and a worthless husband.'

'It's all right, Frank, it's all right. Forget what's gone. Your reactions were understandable. But this morning things just got too much for me.'

'I'm glad Matt came. I never realised before just what he has gone through, now it's made me see things in a different light. Abbe, forgive me.'

'There's nothing to forgive, darling. Please forget it.' She kissed him.

'You were right all along, we can run this ranch. If your pa could, then we can because I'm fortunate in having you.'

Abbe smiled. It was a relief to her Frank talking like this, especially after his attitude throughout the past week. Abbe felt that any setbacks, any depressions would not have the same ominous cloud about them now that Frank's mind would be occupied with the ranch. She must stimulate his interest, keep bolstering it up so that when any setbacks occurred they would be less harmful.

'So we'll prepare for a week's time,' said Abbe.

'No, we run it right now. Your pa said he wasn't going to do any more even though it doesn't become ours officially for another week.'

Abbe smiled to herself. So apart from anything he had said her father had thrown Frank into it. He had to do something.

'Well where do we start?' she asked.

'By appointing a foreman,' replied Frank. 'Get Mike Danvers up here – er that is if you approve of the choice, partner.'

Abbe laughed. 'Anything you say.' She pushed herself to her feet, kissed Frank and rushed from the room. On her way to the outside door she hurried into her father's room where he was sitting looking out of the window. 'Thanks, Dad,' she said and kissed him on the cheek. 'Frank's appointing a new foreman – Mike Danvers, I'm on my way to get him now.'

Matt smiled, so his cajoling had worked. 'A good choice,' he called as Abbe ran from the room.

A few moments later she was showing Mike Danvers into Frank's room.

'Hi, Mike, come in,' Frank greeted.

'Howdy, Mr Hollis, how you feeling?'

'Fine thanks, Mike, if only these legs would go again.'

'They will one day, Mr Hollis.'

Frank smiled wryly. 'I don't expect so Mike but I'm going to run the ranch from here, at least Abigail and I are, but we'll need a good foreman. How about it?'

'Me, Mr Hollis?' gasped a surprised Mike.

'Yes, and look it was Frank when I was a foreman so Frank it still is? I liked what I saw then, you think you're a bit young but you know the job and the men respect you. The job's yours if you want it.'

'Sure do, Frank, thanks for the chance.'

'Right, pull up a chair and we'll start planning. First of all you must feel free to come in here whenever you want to discuss anything just like I did with Mr Clements, right Abbe?'

'Of course,' she replied. 'We'll depend a lot on you Mike until Frank is up and about again. Decisions outside will have to be yours in line with our plans.'

'Right,' replied Mike. 'You can depend on me.'

Mike sat down and, as the two men started to discuss affairs of the ranch, a happy Abigail left the room saying she had a few things to attend to.

Mike Danvers' enthusiasm for his new job infected Frank and at the end of the hour long discussion Frank's interest in the ranch was on the way back to its old fervour.

It was only after Abigail broke up the discussion, saying that Frank had had enough for a first time, that he realised how much it had taken out of him. As the door closed behind Abigail and the new foreman, Frank sank wearily back on the pillows, wondering if he could really cope. He was disappointed that he felt so tired after a mere discussion. For a man who had often spent a day in the saddle, who had urged the men on by his own efforts at branding time, who had ridden the long, arduous, dusty trails of the cattle drive to be tired after talking was no easy thing to take. Frank's thoughts whirled in his uneasy rest. Through the hazy half-dim world of drowsiness, the party, the shot, the paralysis flooded in upon him again. Frank tossed and turned. His legs, he must move his legs, but he couldn't; they were held in a vice-like grip which he couldn't release. That horse was tantalisingly out of his reach, his long supple fingers stretched out but just could not reach the animal, he tried to move forward but couldn't, his legs were holding him back, stopping him from riding and he must ride. Everyone was yelling at him to make the effort; Abigail encouraging, pleading, but most of all Matt shouting, he would do it, he would run the ranch.

Frank woke suddenly, bathed in sweat. He stared about him; the light seemed dimmer in the room. He glanced towards the window and could tell that the sun was lowering towards the west. He must have slept all afternoon. He lay still and thought of his nightmare, of Abbe's efforts during the past week and of Matt's insistence that he was at fault in his attitude.

Ten minutes passed before Abbe looked in and, seeing her husband awake, hurried to the bedside.

'Had a good sleep?' she smiled as she sat on the bed and took Frank's hand.

'Didn't know I'd slept so long.'

'You were fast asleep when I came back after seeing Mike out. Guess all that planning exhausted you.'

'Sure did, but it bothered me – am I going to be able to do it or will it always be like this?'

Abbe smiled. 'Of course it won't always be exhausting; don't forget you're still recovering from a serious wound. You'll find you'll get stronger every day.'

'I hope you're right, Abbe. If only my legs

would get some use in them.'

'They will, darling, they will.' Abbe leaned forward and kissed her husband. She did not want to insist on it too much. She had done this before, trying to convince him and maybe it had had the opposite effect. Now he had got his interest back in the ranch a great deal had been achieved. That interest must be kept up and insistence on walking might detract from it.

Abbe kept it that way throughout the next week. She was delighted with the way Frank's interest in the ranch developed, and he was pleased that his daily session with Mike Danvers became less exhausting. Abigail felt that they were achieving something; Frank's mental attitude was healthy, physically he was getting stronger, the house had settled down to a routine and the ranch was running smoothly once again. The only thing which worried Abbe was the fact that Frank showed no inclination to use his legs. He seemed resigned to the fact that he was paralysed.

Matt stuck to his word, and on the day Abigail and Frank would have been due back from their honeymoon, a fortnight after their wedding day, a lawyer came out from town and the Rocking Chair was legally signed over to them.

Doc Evans paid his daily visit the same afternoon. He was pleased with the news for he felt it could give Frank the mental stimulus he needed to make him walk again. Now might be a good time to try it so, after examining the wound, and being satisfied with it, Doc Evans announced, 'Now, Frank, I figure you can start getting up for a little while each day. We'll keep it to this room for a few days before venturing any further. You can sit in the chair by the window.'

Frank was surprised; the doctor was talking as if he could just get out of bed and walk across to the chair. He must have forewarned Abbe and she must have organised a couple of the hands to come in and carry him to the chair.

'We'll get you sat on the edge of the bed for a start,' said Doc Evans.

Excitedly Abigail turned back the bedclothes and, with the doctor's assistance, got Frank into a sitting position on the edge of the bed.

'Good. Now Frank, think you can walk to the chair if we help you?'

Frank was astounded. What on earth was the doctor talking about? 'You know very well I can't,' replied Frank irritably.

'I know nothing of the sort,' said the

doctor. 'Your legs will feel weak but Abbe and I will help you.'

'Don't talk stupid,' snapped Frank. 'My legs are useless and you know it, so don't mess about. Get a couple of the boys up here to carry me, Abbe.'

'But, Frank, try.' There was anguish in Abbe's eyes and pleading in her voice. She had longed for this moment and had kept hoping that when it came Frank would be determined to try.

'It's no good, Abbe. I'm crippled for life.' There was irritation in every word.

'You're not,' insisted Abigail. She gripped her husband by the shoulders, staring into his eyes. 'You will walk again. You can try now.'

Fran set his mouth in a grim line. He knew that it was no good but it seemed that the only way to prove to Abigail and the doctor that his legs were useless was to try to do what they wanted.

'Come on let me help you,' said Doc Evans putting his arm around Frank's shoulder. He eased him up on to his feet. 'All right, now step forward.'

Frank hesitated, it was as if he was afraid to try.

'Come on, darling,' encouraged Abigail

moving round in front of him and holding her hand out for him to take.

Frank tried but he could not move. Sweat broke out on his forehead. He looked desperately at Abbe and then the doctor who continued to encourage an effort from him.

Try as he would Frank could not make his legs move. A frightened look came into his face but was replaced with such suddenness by one of annoyance and anger that it frightened Abbe. He flung off her hold on his hand, pushed the doctor from him and sank back on the bed.

'There I told you I couldn't,' he snapped angrily. 'You wouldn't listen but I knew I couldn't, I hope you're both satisfied.'

'Frank, Frank, don't talk like that. We did it for your own good, everything we do—'

'Well, don't, it should be obvious I can't and won't walk again,' Frank cut into Abbe's words angrily.

'You will Frank, you will.' Abbe flung her words desperately at her husband hoping to make some impact on his mind. She dropped to her knees beside him gazing into his face with wide tear-filled eyes. 'This is the first try. Another time and you will walk, won't he Doc?' She turned seeking some assurance from him.

'Of course he will. Abbe's right, this is the first time, we'll keep on trying. You can't expect a miracle straight away.'

'That's what it will need to get me right again,' Frank said scornfully. 'Now come on, get me back into bed where this useless hulk should be.'

'You're not useless,' snapped Abigail, anger touching her voice. 'You've proved it this last week by the way the ranch is running. I'll stand no more talk of being useless, if you don't walk again you're not useless. Start thinking like that again and the ranch will run down and if that's going to happen we may as well sell it.'

Frank did not reply and Abbe and the doctor eased him back into bed.

Doc Evans revealed his anxiety to Abigail just before he left.

'I'm pleased with the mental stimulation you are giving Frank and pleased that he has an interest in the ranch. This is good and you must keep it up. But this idea that he is paralysed is firmly planted in his mind. The trouble is getting it out. Coming into his mind in his shocked condition, it played havoc, especially as he was a robust, active man who suddenly saw the exciting outdoor world of a rancher snatched from him, but, as far as I can tell, this paralysis is caused by the imagination, by the mind, and there is no reason why he shouldn't get better, but it will take time and patience on your part and a great deal of determination on Frank's – something which is lacking at the moment. You've got to rekindle that determination, that desire to walk again. If you can do that he will be all right. It's up to you Abbe.'

THREE

Abigail was about to go back into the house as the doctor rode away when she noticed a lone rider round the spur of the hill and head towards the house.

The rider was approaching at a steady trot and in a few moments Abigail recognised him as Carl Petersen. She was pleased, thinking that Carl might be able to ward off some of the depression which Frank was sure to feel after the doctor's abortive attempt to get him to walk.

Abigail waited on the veranda for Carl to arrive. He smiled his pleasure at the sight of her as he pulled his horse to a halt in front of the veranda. Carl swung from the saddle, slipped the reins round the rail and stepped on to the veranda, sweeping his Stetson from his head as he did so.

'Hello, Abbe, nice to see you,' he greeted warmly.

'Hello, Carl,' returned Abbe. There was not the usual zest to her welcome and, although she smiled, Carl sensed that all was not well.

'Something wrong, Abbe?' he asked seriously. 'Is Frank all right? I think that was the doc who just rode off.'

'It was,' replied Abbe. 'Frank's all right except...' She hesitated.

'Except what Abbe?' prompted Carl.

'Doc Evans got him out of bed, tried to make him walk to a chair but Frank couldn't or wouldn't, not even with our help. He says it's all in Frank's mind. Frank is convinced that he won't walk again, and today's episode has come just when he was taking a great interest in the ranch. I'm frightened today might affect the interest, and we'll be back where we started.'

'I'm sorry, Abbe. Anything I can do?'

'Go and see him, Carl. Get his mind off today, back on to the ranch if you can.'

'I'll do what I can, Abbe, anything for the girl who should have married me.' He smiled broadly, but Abbe said nothing as they went into the house. 'Don't bother to come up,' he said when they reached the bottom of the stairs. 'I know the way.'

Abigail watched him as he climbed the stairs wondering what her life would have been like if she had married Carl Petersen. No doubt she would have wanted for nothing, no doubt he would have showered her with everything that money could buy, they would have had the biggest ranch in north Montana with the amalgamation of the Rocking Chair and the Flying Diamond, but she knew she would have missed loving a husband for, although she liked Carl Petersen, Abbe knew she could never have loved him. Already in these last few weeks, in spite of the trouble which had struck, she had experienced more of the delight of deep loving than she could have gained in a lifetime with Carl Petersen.

'Howdy, Frank,' Carl greeted cheerfully as he entered Frank's room.

Frank nodded. He was still battling with the thoughts of his inability to walk. He cursed the doctor for making him try. It brought back vividly something which he already knew but which he had pushed to the back of his mind as he took more and more of an interest in running the ranch. He had become resigned to doing this through Mike Danvers, from his bed; now, after being reminded of his uselessness, he would have to start all over again and reassert his mental attitude towards his position. He must do it for Abbe's sake.

'Hear you've just had the doc,' said Carl as

he sat down beside the bed.

'Fool tried to make me walk,' rapped Frank. 'I never will, so what's the use trying?'

'Well, you never know,' replied Carl. 'Some day you…'

'Don't you start,' interrupted Frank harshly. 'I hope you've come to talk about something better.'

'Sure, Frank, sure. I'm sorry.'

'No need to be. It was only natural. What's the news in town?'

'There's a new singer at the saloon. Pretty hot stuff,' replied Carl.

'And no doubt Carl Petersen will make a play there,' laughed Frank.

'Well, maybe,' Carl grinned, knowing of his reputation as a ladies man. 'I've got to find solace somewhere since you pinched my girl from under my nose.'

Frank smiled. 'All's fair in love and war.'

'Sure is, Frank, sure is,' said Carl thoughtfully.

'Well, there's plenty of other eligible females around Lewistown who'd jump at the chance of marrying you.'

'Maybe, but I wouldn't jump at marrying them. There certainly isn't another Abbe. Reckon I might get right away to find me a wife, like Bob Scammon did.'

'Well, he did all right,' commented Frank.

'Mm,' was Carl's only comment and it was as well that Frank could not read his thoughts.

'You sure would have had a big spread if you'd married Abbe,' said Frank wondering what it would be like to run a ranch the size of the Rocking Chair and Flying Diamond together.

'Yeah,' drawled Carl thoughtfully. 'That's something else I missed out on. It's a challenge I would have liked; so Frank, if ever you think of selling, remember me.'

'Don't reckon that'll happen,' replied Frank. 'Got to have something to hang on to. Can't let Abbe down. Her father ran it from a cripple's chair; I can do it from this bed.' Frank's voice was full of determination.

'Well, you never know how things go,' said Carl. 'If the situation arises where you have to sell, or feel you can't carry on, remember I'll give you a good price.'

'Thanks, Carl,' said Frank. 'I'll give you the first chance.'

Carl smiled to himself. He had extracted a promise and he knew Frank was a man of his word. Now, if pressure could be brought to bear–

'I reckon Frank's got over that upset,' said

Carl to Abbe as he walked into the kitchen.

Abbe turned round from the stove. She smiled with pleasure. 'Thanks, Carl, I'm grateful to you.'

'He's talking and thinking about the ranch again,' said Carl but he did not explain what seeds he had sown.

'Good, I'm pleased about that,' said Abbe. 'I was frightened the...'

'There's no need to be frightened, ever Abbe.' Carl's voice was soft as he stood close to her. 'I'll help all I can, whenever you say so.'

'Thanks, Carl,' replied Abbe. 'It's great to know I've got good friends.' Her hand touched his arm and Carl remembered the times when he had read more in her touch than friendliness. In one swift movement his arms were round her waist pulling her to him and his lips met hers passionately.

Abbe was taken completely by surprise. A moment passed before she struggled and then finally managed to push herself away as Carl's arms relaxed. Her eyes blazed with fury and anger seethed in the tension of her body.

'Don't ever do that again Carl. You–'

'Abbe, I'm sorry, but you were my girl...' cut in Carl.

'I was not,' interrupted Abbe. 'And even if I was it gives you no right to do what you did.'

'You didn't give me a chance, marrying Frank while I was away.'

'You were not my keeper. I didn't have to answer to you.'

'We used to see a lot of each other, maybe not as much during the last six months as we used to but I thought you were still mine.'

'I'm sorry Carl if I misled you. I didn't think we had ever got to the serious stage. Now please, Carl, leave things as they are. We'll forget what's happened and I hope you'll still come here as a friend. I think your visits have helped Frank and I'd like them to continue.'

'All right, I'm sorry Abbe, but this is the first time I've had the opportunity to talk about us since your wedding day.'

'There's nothing to talk about, Carl. I married Frank because I love him and that's all there is to it. Now please leave it.'

'All right, Abbe, but just one thing, I'd still marry you if the opportunity arose.' Carl turned and strode from the room.

Abbe heard him go out of the house and she stood listening to the sound of his horse and thinking of his last words. Then she remembered the outburst of her father on the night of the shooting and began to wonder if he could be right. Was there any connection between that and Carl's words? Was there a hidden threat behind them?

Abbe was suddenly startled by her own thoughts, and she quickly dismissed them as ridiculous. Her father's outburst had been in the hysteria of the moment. He had never mentioned it again so Abbe had not reminded him about it. And as regards a threat from Carl, that was ridiculous, what could he do? Hadn't he helped Frank not hindered him? She was determined to forget the whole incident.

Abigail poured three cups of coffee, took one to her father and the other two along to Frank's room. She was pleased to see him looking much brighter.

'I'm sorry about the doc,' she said.

'Forget it, Abbe,' smiled Frank. 'It was just one of those things.' He was determined not to slip back, not to be upset by the un-fruitful effort to walk. 'It's only natural that you all expected me to walk but I know I never will, so there it is. I'm sorry I blew up but after the strain and tension well–. I've forgotten it so let's not talk of it again.'

Abbe kissed him. 'Have a good chat with Carl?' she asked.

'Yes,' replied Frank. 'You know some of the things we talked about made me wonder if we wouldn't be better selling the Rocking Chair and finding somewhere smaller, more manageable, capable of being run by a couple of men.'

Abigail was so taken aback by the unexpected suggestion that she did not speak for a few moments. This idea could only have come from Carl. He may well have got Frank's mind back on the ranch but he had put in a suggestion which could only have been for his own ends. Abbe was beginning to have second thoughts about Carl Petersen.

'Rubbish,' she said, 'we're managing all right. We have a good system running smoothly. There'd be no point in moving to a smaller place you'd still have to run it from your bed so you may as well keep the bigger spread.'

'I was only thinking of taking some of the worry off your shoulders, Abbe.'

'That's a nice thought but forget it. I'm all right. Besides this is our ranch, and our ranch I want it to remain, and don't forget it has always been my home, I don't want to leave it.'

'All right, all right,' said Frank trying to smooth down Abigail's indignation. 'Forget it.'

'I suppose Carl's given you this idea.'

'Well partly, he said if ever we wanted to sell he'd buy.'

'Don't forget in this case it takes three to make a bargain, and I'll not sell my half of the ranch unless it becomes absolutely necessary and that point will take some reaching. I thought Carl's visits were good for you but now I wonder. Maybe I'd better tell him not to call again.'

'No, you can't do that Abbe. There's no cause, he's our neighbour and he's done what he could to help since the shooting.'

Abigail was on the point of telling Frank what had happened in the kitchen but thought better of it. It would only upset Frank again and she didn't want that.

During the next two weeks the question of selling the ranch never came up again and it receded in Frank's mind as he became more and more immersed in the affairs of the Rocking Chair. True he had fits of depression when he was alone, when the impact of being unable to walk, of feeling helpless, made itself particularly felt. If only he could get about and see what was happening. He trusted Mike Danvers implicitly and the young cowboy seemed to be dealing with his new responsibilities effectively, but Frank wanted to be amongst the activity, to be part of it and play his full share as he once had done.

But, for Abbe's sake, Frank kept his desires to himself. He did not want to upset her again as he once had done. He realised he owed a great deal to her; he knew how hard things must be for her, and he did not want to make an added burden of his own feelings. She wanted him to play as full a part as possible in the running of the ranch, and he was determined to do so to please her.

Doc Evans did not immediately approach the subject of walking again but he suggested that Frank got out of bed to sit by the window, extending the time each day. Frank with his new attitude of mind welcomed this. Sitting was a change from laying and he felt on more equal terms when Mike Danvers visited him.

One day Doc Evans arrived just after Frank had had a particularly exhilarating time with Mike Danvers. The foreman had reported the stock in good condition with an exceptional number of cows calving. Four horse wranglers had brought in what promised to be a profitable bunch of wild horses. The horses would bring a good price from the Army, and the good birth rate augered well for the future herds.

Doc Evans sensed Frank's mood and thought this would be the right time to bring up the subject of walking.

After giving Frank his usual check-up the doctor looked hard at him. 'Now, Frank, I'm going to tell you once again that I can't see any physical reason why you aren't walking again. How about giving it another go?'

'Aw, come off it, Doc,' said Frank. 'I've had a good day, don't spoil it.'

'This could make it better.'

'I can't walk,' replied Frank.

'You don't know that until you try.'

Frank looked at Abbe who said nothing. She wanted this to be his own choice. She felt it had to come from him, it had to be something he wanted to do. Although Abigail had never mentioned the subject for some time, Frank knew that she nurtured the belief that some day he would walk again. For her sake he must make the effort, he must try even though it would be no good.

'All right let's have a go!'

Relief and pleasure flowed through Abigail and she smiled encouragingly as she came beside her husband.

'Good,' the doctor beamed enthusiastically. 'We'll help you to stand then it's up to you.'

Abigail and the doctor helped Frank to his feet. He stood awkwardly, holding, with one hand, on to the table to balance on legs he felt were useless. The doctor moved two yards in front of him.

'Come on, now come to me,' he said quietly but firmly. Abigail took her husband's free arm. 'No, Abbe, leave him,' said the doctor. 'Let him try on his own. Come on Frank.'

Frank's lips tightened. He tried to move his legs, tried to give them a message from his brain but they took no notice. Sweat broke out on his forehead as he tried harder and harder. The doctor watched him anxiously, his body tensed almost as if he was trying to walk for him. Abbe bit her lip anxiously as the words 'Walk, Frank, walk,' thundered time and again through her mind.

Frank's effort mounted and mounted, his face creased and twisted as he tried to force his legs to move. Then suddenly he could take no more and he relaxed, almost losing his balance as he did so. The doctor and Abbe sprang to his side supporting him and then slowly lowered him into his chair. 'There, it's hopeless; I will never walk,' he said despondently.

Abigail was disappointed. The hope of success had been dashed. Only one thing consoled her, there had been no outburst as there was last time and in this she saw a certain victory. Making the effort and failing had not had the shattering effect it had had before.

'All right, Frank, relax,' said the doctor. Abigail mopped the sweat from his forehead. 'At least we've made a try and if we periodically have a go we may succeed one day. In the meantime I have a suggestion.' He looked at Abbe. 'Would it be possible to make a room for Frank downstairs?'

'Yes,' replied Abigail, puzzled by the reason for the question.

'In that case I suggest I get Frank a wheelchair.'

'Wheelchair! Not for me I'm not going to be seen as a helpless cripple.' Frank's outburst startled Abbe.

'But Frank, you'll be able to get about more,' she said.

'No wheelchair for me!'

'Frank be reasonable,' put in the doctor. 'Look, I'm convinced that one day you will walk again, but you aren't. So if you are right, what are you going to do? Stay in this room all the time? Have a wheelchair and you'll not be confined to this room, you'll be able to move about downstairs and get outside. You could have ramps made to enable you to negotiate the veranda steps.'

Abigail's eyes sparkled at the prospect. 'Think of it Frank,' she took up the doctor's persuasive talk enthusiastically, 'you'd be able to get out, see the men, be more a part of running the ranch.'

'And how do you think I'd feel,' retorted Frank, 'being there, being close to the corral fence when they're breaking-in horses, bringing in the cattle, jobs I used to do? How do you think it would be watching stuck in a wheelchair.'

'Probably the same way as I sometimes feel now,' Abbe's voice was sharp with a touch of annoyance to it. 'You know how I loved to ride, how I liked to be in the open, how I liked the ranch life. Frank, your accident, took those things away from me just as much as they took them from you.' Abbe's voice faltered, she stared at Frank, horrified at herself for hitting back in front of someone. Tears started to fill her eyes. She turned apologetically to the doctor. 'I'm sorry I–'

'That's all right, Abbe,' replied Doc Evans. 'It will have done you good to get it off your mind.' He stared at Frank. 'Abbe's right you know, it will make life much more open and interesting for you both.'

Frank was staring at Abbe. He did not speak for a moment then held out his hand to her. 'I'm sorry, Abbe,' he said quietly. 'I didn't realise.'

Abbe squeezed his hand affectionately. 'I know,' she said, 'there are things you don't see and tend to lose touch with when you're in this room all day.' She leaned forward and kissed him lightly on the cheek. 'I'm sorry for my outburst.'

'No, no, don't be sorry, Abbe, it brought something to me.' He looked up at he doctor. 'Right, well give it a try.'

Abbe smiled, forcing back the tears. 'When will you want the room ready?'

'Tomorrow too soon?'

Abbe shook her head. 'No, we'll start on it right away.'

The doctor accompanied Abigail from the room. 'I'm doing this for two reasons,' he explained. 'It will enable Frank to become much more involved in the ranch and therefore have more to occupy his mind and time and will get him among more people.'

'You don't think Frank will get too dependent on the chair and lose the desire to walk?' queried Abbe.

'I doubt it,' reassured Doc Evans. 'If he gets out among the men I'm hoping it will stimulate his desire to walk again. Seeing the men active with horses and cattle could just provide that something which is missing right now.'

'Let's hope you're right,' said Abigail. 'Thanks for what you're doing.'

Doc Evans smiled. 'I only wish it was more. I wish I could convince him he could walk. Keep trying, Abbe, a lot depends on you.'

When the doctor had gone Abigail set about preparing a room downstairs for Frank, and before long his bed was taken down and two of the hands carried Frank to his new surroundings. Once he was settled in he rather liked the change and enjoyed the sense or being nearer things, of not being cut off upstairs.

The following morning Doc Evans was at the Rocking Chair early and soon had Frank in the wheelchair in his room. A few movements and he soon got the hang of manoeuvring it on his own. Anticipating that Frank would want to venture outside as soon as he was mobile Abbe had had two of the hands make the necessary ramps.

Helped by Abigail's guiding hands Frank negotiated the doorways successfully. He slowed and stopped when he reached the veranda. He glanced round, a smile breaking across his face as he breathed deeply of the fresh, clear, Montana air. It was good to feel the gentle breeze playing around his face again as the world took on new and brighter horizons.

Mike Danvers who was hurrying from the bunk-house towards a pole-fenced corral which held several horses spotted Frank. He broke into a trot. 'The boss!' he called to the ranch-hands who were preparing to cut-out one of the horses. They all hurried after Mike, smiles of pleasure on their weather-tanned faces.

'Howdy, Frank,' greeted Mike with a grin. 'Mighty good to see you out again.'

'Thanks, Mike, it sure feels great,' said Frank, who went on to acknowledge the greetings of the welcoming cowboys as they gathered round the ramp from the veranda.

He looked up at Abbe and smiled. 'Let's

feel that nice Montana sun,' he said and started to ease himself forward towards the ramp.

Abbe maintained a steadying hand and the cowboys raised a cheer as Frank negotiated the ramp and reached ground baked hard by the long hot summer.

Frank felt as if new life was being driven into him as the sun beat on his skin, paled by his confinement.

The doctor came down the steps. 'Now, Frank you can get about among the men and see what they are doing.'

Frank smiled. 'Thanks, Doc.' There was an appreciation for all that the doctor had done in Frank's voice.

'I've done very little, Frank. I want to see you walk again. Don't get stuck in that wheelchair. I'll be out tomorrow to see how you get on.'

'All right come on you men let the boss see how you can handle those horses.' Mike spoke with authority and the men made their way back to the corral as the doctor climbed into his buggy and drove off. 'Like to have a look round, Frank?' asked the foreman.

'Sure would.'

Abbe was pleased with Frank's enthusiasm and she silently thanked the doctor for suggesting the wheelchair. She only hoped Frank's keenness would not be set back when he saw the men in action. The testing time would soon come.

As Mike Danvers began to push the chair Abbe fell into step beside Frank. She felt his hand reach out and take hers firmly but gently. She felt a love in his touch which she returned.

Frank was pleased with what he saw and what his foreman told him as they went around. The fences and the buildings were all in good repair, the stable had been extended as Frank planned, the wagons and two buggies were well maintained and all the riding horses were in tip-top condition.

'You're doing a good job, Mike,' Frank commented.

'Thanks, boss.'

'Right, let's see these mustangs you brought in.'

Mike pushed him over to the corral which held the twenty horses. They found that Matt had struggled over from the house and was leaning on the corral fence casting an expert eye over the livestock. He turned as they approached. 'It's mighty good to see you outside again, Frank,' said Matt.

'And it's mighty good to be out,' replied Frank with a grin. 'You want to get yourself one of these contraptions, Matt.'

'Not me. Fine idea for you, but my complaint's different. Get into one of those and I'll seize up altogether. Got to keep my old bones creaking even though it takes an effort. Doc wanted me to have one some time ago, I said I would when the time came. I'll use it all right, they'll never hog-tie me to the house.'

Frank smiled. He had been viewing the horses as his father-in-law spoke. 'What do you think of them?' he asked.

Matt turned back to lean on the fence and survey the animals. He held his counsel for a moment, then said 'Good looking lot.'

'Three on the thin side and one with a slight limp,' commented Frank.

'Yeah,' agreed Matt, pleased that Frank's sight for horses had lost none of its keenness.

'Should make a good price when you've worked them, Mike,' said Frank.

'Try the black with the blaze,' called Mike.

Four men who had entered the corral swiftly and expertly cut out the required horse as the animals turned and moved trying to escape the determined humans. The men worked the black towards the sliding gate which was opened at the right moment to admit the horse into a smaller corral.

Immediately a tall slim man advanced towards the horse which twisted and turned to try to keep away. Frank watched the scene intently as the ranch's horse wrangler expertly manoeuvred himself into a position from which he could bring his lariat into use. Suddenly the rope snaked out and the lasso entwined itself round the black's forefeet. With a swift precise movement the horse wrangler brought the animal to the ground.

Three men who had been waiting beside the rails, ran forward. Two of them sat on the horse's head while the third, a short stocky cowboy, the professional bronc-buster, who usually worked this part of Montana and was well known to the Rocking Chair men, slipped a hackamore on to the horse's head. The black snorted and twitched but was held firm by the two men who as soon as the hackamore was on covered the horse's fiery eyes with their Stetsons. Holding their hats in position the two men allowed the animal to get up.

Frank was tense watching the horse's reaction but with its eyes covered it remained quiet. The bronc-buster tucked the long mecate into his belt so that he would be able to mount the horse with the ropes ready for use. A cowboy who had come over with a lightweight bronc saddle helped the buster to saddle the horse quickly. While the men at the horse's head kept it steady the bronc-buster climbed into the saddle. He untucked the mecate from his belt and held it firmly in his right hand. One last brief moment of settling himself then he yelled 'Let him go!'

As if they were one the two cowboys whisked their Stetsons away from the black's eyes and ran for the rails.

Immediately its eyes were uncovered the strong, wiry horse leaped into the air and as soon as it thudded to the ground it was into the air again. It bucked and twisted in its attempts to remove the unwanted man from its back.

After the first few minutes of silence the men around the corral started shouting encouragement to the rider.

'Stick to him!'

'Ride him, Jim!'

'Tame the critter!'

Frank's knuckles were white as he gripped the arms of his chair, his concentration focussed hard on the twisting, turning mass of horseflesh. The bronc-buster, his left arm held out to keep his balance, rode with every movement of the horse, the long mecate giving the animal's head plenty of play which a shorter bridle wouldn't have allowed.

Suddenly the horse pulled up sharply and stood still. The cowboys yelled their approval of the buster's success but he was not to be fooled. He was alert, ready for the black's next move. He knew this animal wasn't played out yet.

Abigail smiled at Frank. 'He's a beauty,' she whispered to him. 'Jim rode him well.'

As if it had heard her the black suddenly leapt into the air. All four legs seemed to have springs in them. He arched his back leaving Jim with precious little to sit on. As soon as all four hoofs tore the earth again the back legs came off the ground but the buster counteracted the attempt to pitch him off by a sway of his body. When his back legs struck the ground the black immediately reared almost catching Jim unawares by the swiftness of the change. A gasp went up from the watchers who had been caught completely by surprise at the black's extra effort to unseat the man on his back.

There was a swirl of dust, a tearing of the soil, man and horse were almost a blur.

Gradually the black's efforts became less vicious then suddenly before anyone realised what was happening the horse leaped into the air and at the same time twisted sharply round to face the opposite direction as it pounded into the ground.

The manoeuvre caught Jim who, sensing he had won, relaxed for that moment for which the black was waiting. The viciousness of the move flung him hard from the saddle. He crashed heavily and awkwardly to the ground. The spectators cried out. Two men were swiftly away from the coral rails, ropes were ready. But the horse evaded them and bound back towards the still figure of Jim. Mike Danvers was racing towards him.

As the horse turned back Frank yelled, 'Look out Mike!' The voice was so shrill, so fierce that Abbe, whose attention had been absorbed by the happenings inside the fence turned. She gasped. Frank was on his feet!

In the excitement and without realising it, Frank had pulled himself up from his chair and now he was standing, holding tightly to the rail and yelling at Mike.

Mike reached Jim before the stallion but had no time to get him out of the way. Mike jumped between Jim and the horse sweeping his black Stetson from his head as he did so.

The stallion slid to a halt frightened by the waving arms and flapping Stetson. Dust swirled and, snorting loudly, the animal reared up on its hind-legs with its forelegs flaying at the air. As its hooves crashed downwards on to the hard ground the two cowboys quickly closed alongside it and turned it away.

Mike turned and dropped on his knees beside the unconscious man. In a moment other cowboys were beside him and, raising him gently, they carried him from the corral as Mike shouted for someone to ride after Doc Evans.

As the men came out of the corral Frank, whose attention had been riveted on the happening, relaxed and was suddenly aware that he was standing. He glanced round sharply at Abbe who read in his eyes a helplessness, a fear of a situation in which he had been caught unawares and with which he couldn't cope. She saw an almost child-like plea for help.

Abigail smiled as she stepped to him. 'Frank, you got up on your own. It's wonderful.' Her voice reflected her delight in what her husband had achieved, trying to instill a confidence in him. 'Do you want to try to walk?'

The sweat began to drop from Frank's forehead. He felt hot and clammy as he gripped the rail tightly, nervous as to what would happen if he let go.

'No. No. Get me back in the chair, quick.'

Abigail pushed the chair back to Frank who flopped into it as Abigail held it steady. He heaved a big sigh, fumbled for his handkerchief, mopped his forehead and wiped his brow.

'Whew. I hope I never find myself in a situation like that again,' he said.

'You were all right,' Abigail's voice was soft and comforting. 'It was a great step forward, next time you'll be able to stand without holding the rail.' She did not want to press the matter too far and was pleased that Mike Danvers was approaching them.

'How's Jim?' asked Frank, as Mike climbed the fence.

'I don't like the look of his shoulder,' replied Mike.

'Take me over to the bunk-house, please. I'd like to be on hand when the doc gets back.'

Abbe started to push Frank but Mike took over and they were on hand when Doc Evans returned. He made a quick examination of Jim, who had regained consciousness, pronounced him all right except for a dislocated shoulder which he put back and strapped up with instructions to take things quietly for a few days.

As Frank was in deep conversation with his foreman and some of the hands, Abigail took the opportunity to tell the doctor about Frank getting up from his wheelchair.

Doctor Evans looked thoughtful as he listened but when Abbe had finished her story he seemed pleased.

'It bears out what I believe,' he said. 'This is something largely mental, look at his reaction when he realised what he had done. I hoped something like this would happen when he got out among the men. It's happened quicker than I expected. The more he gets out the better.' He glanced in the direction of Frank. 'He certainly is throwing himself wholeheartedly into the ranch now.'

Abigail smiled. 'Thanks to you.' She bade the doctor good-bye and returned to her husband who was still talking to Mike, the other cowboys having returned to continue the work with the horses.

'Abbe,' said Frank when she reached them, 'I'd like you to ride over to the north range with Mike and have a look at the cattle there. Mike tells me they're in good condition but he doubts the wisdom of selling this year.'

'But I can't go, Frank. What about you? Besides–' she objected but Frank cut her short.

'It'll be all right. If I want to go back into the house one of the men will take me, but Matt and I will be all right together; we'll be watching the horse wrangling for a while.'

'I don't think I–' started Abbe again.

'Now there's no reason why you can't go so don't start looking for one. Off you go; it will do you good.'

Abbe smiled. She knew Frank had purposely worked this out with Mike but she didn't let on she had seen through his ruse. It would be marvellous to be in the saddle again, to ride across the range and feel the wind and sun. 'All right,' she said. 'I won't be long, Mike.'

She started towards the house but stopped as Carl Petersen rode up. He pulled his horse to a halt in front of Frank.

'Howdy,' he greeted with a smile which embarrassed all three. Abigail watched him carefully but when their eyes met as he swung from the saddle he showed no embarrassment at the thought of what had happened between them the last time they had met.

'Well,' he went on, 'this is sure a fine sight to see you outside, Frank, and mobile at that.'

Frank grinned. 'I was forgetting what the wind and the sun were like.'

'You'll never know where you have him now, Abbe,' said Carl with a grin.

'This is just what he wanted,' said Abbe. 'Frank will certainly be able to play a more active part in running the ranch.'

Abbe knew the pointedness of her words were not lost on Carl. He realised that there was less chance of persuading Frank to sell the Rocking Chair now.

'That's great,' said Carl contrary to his real feelings. Ten minutes later when he rode away he was already formulating some plan to force the Rocking Chair and Hash Knife his way.

Persuasion would be useless; action was necessary.

FOUR

Frank and Matt were sitting on the veranda when Abigail and Mike returned from the ride to the north part of the Rocking Chair.

Matt watched Frank carefully as the riders approached. He was afraid Frank might be upset by the sight of them, particularly of Abbe riding, when he was confined to his wheelchair and limited to the vicinity of the ranch-house. If any thought of regret, of self-pity crossed Frank's mind he did not show it, and all Matt saw was admiration and love for Abbe.

Frank was glad he had found a reason to get Abbe back into the saddle, he knew how she loved riding, loved the open air ranch life and he realised how hard it must have been for her to stay cooped up in the house since his accident. And he knew that as long as he was confined to the house she would not resume the activities she loved. Now that he was mobile, able to get around outside, she would probably be more inclined to ride more often. Frank was determined to see that she did.

'Enjoy that?' asked Frank as she swung gracefully from the saddle.

'Mm,' Abbe flashed her pleasure in a smile. She tipped her low-crowned, grey sombrero from her head so that it hung down her back by its cord. She came up the steps and flopped into a chair beside Frank, taking his hand as she did so. 'Been all right, darling?'

'Sure,' replied Frank. 'What are the cattle like?'

'Good bunch, aren't they Mike?'

The foreman agreed as he leaned against the rail.

'Well, keep or sell Abbe?'

Abbe looked thoughtful for a moment. 'Well, seeing that prices are down this year I figure it might be best to hold on to them. Some could do with fattening up and if prices go up next year then we could see a good profit.'

Frank glanced at his father-in-law. 'What do you think, Matt?'

'It's your ranch. I said I would not inter-fere. You two make your own decisions and stand by them, right or wrong,' replied Matt.

Frank smiled and looked at Abbe. 'Hold?'

Abbe nodded.

'Right, Mike you can plan accordingly,' instructed Frank.

'Sure, boss,' said Mike. He glanced at Abbe. 'I'll take your horse over to the stable.'

'Thanks,' replied Abbe.

Mike left then, leading the two horses to the stable where he tended to his own while the stableman saw to Abbe's.

Ten minutes later Abigail was still sitting talking to Frank and her father when Bob and Nancy Scammon rode up.

'Well, this is sure a good sight,' boomed Bob. 'All of you outside.' His saddle creaked as it was relieved of his weight when he swung to the ground.

'And to see Abbe dressed for riding,' added Nancy with obvious pleasure when she stepped into the shade of the veranda.

'When did you get this?' asked Bob indicating the wheelchair as he brought some chairs for Nancy and himself.

'Just this morning, Bob,' said Frank. 'First time out and it's great.'

'Good, you can get about and see more of the ranch.' Bob's deep voice showed his delight that Frank could lead a more interesting life.

'And with you more occupied, Frank, maybe I can see a bit more of Abbe at the

Hash Knife,' suggested Nancy.

'That's just what I was saying, Nancy. I want Abbe to get out and about again,' Frank replied.

'Then restart your visits,' Nancy smiled at Abbe. There was no doubting her delight that some of the old routine would return to her friend's life.

Abbe smiled at them all. 'I'll look forward to that, but don't expect me as much as I used to, well not until Frank's up and about again.'

The conversation drifted through everyday topics for about ten minutes when Abigail suggested that she get them all a drink.

Nancy accompanied Abbe into the house and the men turned to ranch talk.

'I'm glad you came over, Bob, I wanted to see you about this year's drive,' said Frank.

'Wal, I was thinking of missing out this year, but I was a bit bothered in case it was letting you down seeing that we usually join up for the drive to the railhead.'

Frank grinned. 'I was thinking just the same so now no one's put out.'

'Good,' beamed Bob, obviously relieved that he was not letting down old friends.

Abbe and Nancy returned with the cooling drinks and a few minutes later they were attracted by the sound of an approaching horse.

When greetings had been exchanged with Sheriff Bill Mathews Matt put a straight question.

'Got any leads yet?'

Although it was a general query, the sheriff realised that what Matt really wanted to know was if he had got any leads on Carl Petersen.

Bill shook his head. 'Afraid not and there isn't much chance now unless the would-be killer tries again. Maybe we could push him into it.'

'What do you mean?' asked Frank, voicing the question which had sprung to everyone's mind.

'Wal, I heard from Doc Evans that Frank had got a wheelchair; a mighty good idea and I'm pleased to see you out again Frank. Wal, I figured with you more in the open the killer might try again especially if we gave him tempting bait.'

'Oh! No!' The gasp came from Abbe. 'No, Bill, Frank's not going to lay himself open–'

She leaned forward in her chair, concern and anguish on her face as she nervously fingered her glass.

Frank placed a comforting hand on her

arm. 'Let's hear what Bill has to say.'

'Give another party, say it's the continuation of the wedding party. Set up the situation again, only this time we'll be waiting for him.' The sheriff, wanting comment, glanced at the three men.

'It's a good idea,' said Matt, 'but a bit risky.'

'Sure there's a risk to it but it's less risky than not knowing when he might strike,' said Bill. 'Wal, Frank?'

Frank glanced at his wife. She was about to comment but desisted when she felt the pressure of Frank's hand.

'You think if we create a similar situation the killer might try again.'

'Yes. Such a situation gives him more opportunity.'

'And you will be waiting for him.'

'Yes. Look, as I figure it he must use the trees as cover. Anywhere else would be tricky because he wouldn't have such ease of getaway. Look at it for yourselves.'

They all saw the sheriff's point when they studied the lie of the land before the house and recalled the shooting.

'Now given the knowledge that he must try from the trees, I and my deputies will be waiting.'

Frank nodded. 'Sounds feasible.'

'But Frank you're putting yourself at risk,' protested Abigail.

'Maybe,' agreed Frank, 'but if it means catching the killer I'm all for it.'

'Oh, no.' Tears came to Abbe's eyes. 'What – what if he succeeds?' The words almost choked in Abigail's throat as she thought of the consequences.

'He won't, darling, the sheriff will be there.' Frank tried to offer his wife some comfort.

'Dad, Dad, please don't let them do it.'

The anguished plea from his daughter tore at Matt but he held his mind firm. 'I'd said I'd not interfere in anything but I figure this is one time when I might do just that.' A certain relief flowed in Abbe; her father agreed with her; but that was dashed as he went on. 'I'm all for catching the killer as soon as possible and if this will do it then I'm all for it,' Abigail gasped. She had expected support from her father. He looked sympathetically at her. 'It's because I'm afraid of what might happen if he isn't caught, that I go along with the idea.'

Abigail jumped from her chair, tears streaming down her face, and, with Nancy close behind her friend ready to comfort her, ran into the house.

Frank started to pull himself up from his wheelchair, wanting to go to his wife to be some help to her. Matt, Bob and the sheriff stared at him in surprise. Was this incident going to be the compelling force to make him walk? Was the fact that he wanted to be a comfort to his wife in her moments of anguish going to be of such intensity that it would break down the mental barrier?

Frank was half way up when he realised what he was doing and his mind told him it would be no good if he stood up for he could not walk. He flopped back in his chair, and glanced quickly at his friends and was thankful that they appeared not to have noticed what he had done.

As Frank sat down again Matt and Bob exchanged looks of disappointment and the sheriff turned to gaze towards the door.

'She'll be all right,' assured Bob. 'Nancy will take care of her.'

'Yes, I know,' said Frank and turned the conversation back to instrumenting the sheriff's plan.

A quarter of an hour later, when Abbe and Nancy returned, all arrangements had been made.

'I'm sorry,' Abbe apologised. She went to Frank and laid a hand on his shoulder.

'Please do what you think is best.'

He took her hand reassuringly. 'We've fixed the party for a week tonight,' he explained. 'If invitations could go out to exactly the same people who were at the wedding party. Maybe Nancy would–'

'Of course, I'll help in any way I can,' Nancy broke in. 'What about making plans now, Abbe?'

Abbe nodded. 'Best get started as soon as possible.'

'Not a word to anyone about this,' warned the sheriff. 'This plan is known to only six of us. I won't even tell my deputies what's happening until the night of the party.'

The invitations went out that next day and Carl Petersen smiled when he received his. This was giving him an opportunity he hadn't bargained for. Now he could work things his way sooner than he expected.

A week later, the oil lamps, hung from the poles in front of the Rocking Chair ranch-house, were lit as the clear Montana sky darkened to leave a myriad of stars making a perfect canopy for the pleasant gathering of friends. While the atmosphere could never be the same as on that first occasion, it was, nevertheless, happy and enjoyable. Matt, sitting in his chair in the same place at the foot of the steps, had a companion this time in Frank, who positioned his wheelchair next to his father-in-law. Guests, as they were greeted by Frank and Abbe, did not mention the tragic happening at the last party, nor did they offer any sympathy to Frank, for they knew it might only raise regrets in a man who was coping effectively with what could have been a crushing disability, and who was carrying out an active life in a new way.

The last week had seen Frank adapt himself rapidly to the greater freedom offered by the wheelchair, and Abbe, delighted with his progress, was much easier in her mind. Frank, at least, had conquered the mental depression and upset she had feared. Frank had insisted that Abbe should no longer tie herself as much to the ranch and accordingly, with the party to be organised, she had ridden over to the Hash Knife several times to see Nancy. The only blot on the whole week for her had been that, at the back of her mind, there was the fear of the risk Frank would be taking in setting himself up as a target for a would-be killer.

She was nervous as the guests arrived in spite of Frank's efforts at reassurance before they left the house. However, in the short moments of greeting, no one detected her feelings.

Soon the party was in full swing. Gingham frocks and tailed coats swirled in the last strong light from a clear Montana sky, keeping in time with the three man band on the veranda. Abigail was reluctant to leave Frank's side but she had to mingle with the guests and she could hardly refuse dance after dance especially when Frank encouraged her to accept the invitations. When Abigail danced with Bob she felt some reassurance at the presence of her good friends, but she knew they could not prevent what she feared was inevitable.

The light was starting to fade when Abigail danced with Carl Petersen. She felt more in his touch than mere guidance through the dance, and she knew he still hoped that one day she would be his. Good manners prevented her from breaking away and she could hardly reprimand him now. That could be done later.

'Nice idea continuing the wedding party,' remarked Carl. 'I was surprised when I got the invitation, I thought Frank – but he seems to be enjoying himself in spite of being stuck in that wheelchair.'

'We've got to live as normal a life as possible,' pointed out Abbe. 'Frank was all for this.'

'Did every wedding guest accept?'

'Yes.'

'Then I must have missed Bill Mathews. Strange I haven't seen his deputies either.'

'Oh, I think they are somewhere about,' replied Abbe quickly.

'I must have missed them. Thought they might be on a case when I hadn't seen any of them.'

Abbe was flustered. She was annoyed with herself for answering too quickly. It would seem strange to Carl that she had seen them and he hadn't. She felt her cheeks redden and she hoped Carl didn't notice.

Carl felt Abbe's reply was evasive. He sensed that there was something odd about the fact that all the original guests except all the lawmen were there. It was also odd that Abigail indicted she had seen them, after all she had received the guests on their arrival, and now she made no comment on his last observation. Carl felt uneasy, he quickly changed the topic of conversation even though his mind was still on the missing lawmen.

He had been alert to every possibility since arriving at the party; he had his plans made but he had to be sure everything was right to ensure their fulfilment. At first he had been satisfied; Frank was in almost the same position as last time but then Carl began to think that everything was too right. Frank had never moved from his place close to the veranda steps and Carl had expected him to move around among the guests. Something began to nag at Carl and he checked everything again. It came as a shock when he realised that the sheriff and his deputies were not at the party. Now Abigail's attitude made him even more suspicious.

The dance finished. Carl thanked Abigail and escorted her back to Frank. He waited a moment and them made his excuses. Abigail watched him go to the table from which the drinks were being served.

She felt a little uneasy at Carl's queries about the lawmen but the enquiry could have been quite legitimate with no ulterior motive. Her father's outburst after the shooting came back to her mind. Was there something in it? It had never been mentioned again but–.

Abbe's thoughts were broken by the conversation around her as Nancy and Bob joined them. For a few moments her attention was directed away from Carl Petersen and when she looked back to the table Carl had gone! Near panic seized Abigail. She glanced round anxiously, telling herself that her feelings were foolish, bred on thoughts which had got the better of her. Nevertheless, relief swept over her when she saw Carl's dark hair among the crowd near the end of the house. Although she was telling herself everything was all right she found that she was keeping Carl under observation.

Suddenly Abigail tensed herself. She saw Carl slip away from the crowd and pass beyond her sight along the side of the house. Why had Carl left the gathering especially to go along the side of the house? Abigail's curiosity was raised.

Abigail quickly made an excuse to go into the house and after strolling casually inside she hurried through to the back door. She opened it quietly so that she could just see through the narrow opening. A shadowy figure walked quickly through the gloom. Abigail stepped outside. She glanced around and, seeing no one else, followed Carl Petersen, keeping at a discreet distance.

Petersen quickened his pace and Abbe began to find it difficult to keep him in sight. She saw him cross the main track from the ranch and take a path through the trees which cut out a curve in the track as it swung towards the ford across the river. The path cut across the edge of the wood and Abbe realised Carl would not be seen by the lawmen as this was a section from which a gunman could not get Frank in his sights.

Abigail hurried forward but, by the time she reached the trees, Carl was not to be seen. She hurried along, but saw no sign of him by the time she reached the main track again. Petersen must have left the path; if he had gone to his right the lawmen would see him but he could be anywhere in the thickets on the left. She retraced her steps with only the sigh of the pines, touched by the gentle breeze, coming from the wood. Beyond, the music floated on the night air. The happy carefree atmosphere contrasted heavily with the tenseness Abigail had built up around her. Had she been right in following Petersen or were her suspicions unfounded? She realised she had proved nothing.

When she reached the house she used the back door and as she stepped out on to the veranda at the front she pulled up sharply with surprise. Carl Petersen was dancing past with Nancy! He smiled up at her, and Abigail wondered if she detected a slight mockery in that smile. Had he known she was following him? Or was she reading things which weren't meant? She moved down the steps to stand beside Frank.

He looked up and smiled. 'All right, honey?'

'Yes, thanks,' she nodded, but he detected a nervousness.

He took her hand. 'I'll be all right,' he reassured her.

The moments passed slowly. A dance finished and Nancy rejoined them. As the band started the next number Frank felt a moment in time which had happened before. But no shot came and the moment passed. Dance after dance went on. Then Carl Petersen was in front of them, flashing a smile and bowing a request to Nancy for another dance. She accepted and was whisked away in a whirl of dancers.

The nagging minutes passed. There was a tension in the group at the foot of the veranda steps. The half-expected shot, the desired shout from the lawmen never came.

As the evening wore on, Frank became more relaxed, Matt felt annoyed that the sheriff's plan did not seem to be working, Bob felt less tense than he had done all evening, Abigail still showed her apprehension, and Nancy felt uneasy for her friend.

Two hours later the first guests began to leave and by another hour all the guests had gone leaving behind their thanks for a highly successful party which they had enjoyed enormously. It was only when the final guest had gone and he had seen Frank go into the house that Sheriff Bill Mathews dismissed his deputies and made his way to the house.

'Sorry my idea didn't work,' he said when he joined Frank. 'There's been no one in the wood tonight.'

'It was worth a try,' commented Frank. 'Maybe there won't be another attempt to kill me.'

It seemed that Frank was right for ranch-life drifted back into a normality which was broken a week later when Mike Danvers came in from the north range.

Frank and Matt were on the veranda when Mike breasted a rise to the right of the ranch and attracted the attention by the swiftness of his approach.

Frank glanced at Matt. 'Mike's sure in a hurry.'

'Yeah,' Matt grunted, frowning at the prospect of trouble which he read into Mike's fast gallop.

The sound of the hard ridden horse brought Abigail hurrying out of the house. One glance told her it was their foreman.

'Wasn't Mike going to the north range?' she asked, looking at Frank.

'Sure, but something's bringing him back in a mighty hurry.'

Dust swirled beneath the horse's hooves as Mike hauled on the reins bringing it to a halt in front of the veranda.

'Rustlers!' he shouted as he pulled the horse round and steadied it.

'What!' A gasp of surprise came from the three people.

Mike swung out of the saddle and on to the veranda to find his boss anxious for his explanation.

'I reckon about fifty head are missing from the north range,' said Mike, 'and definite signs of a number of riders in the vicinity.'

'You sure, Mike? There hasn't been rustlin' around here for years,' said Matt.

'Wal, I've given you the evidence as I saw it,' explained Mike. 'I sent Red and Hal to see if they could find a trail.'

'Good,' said Frank. His fingers twitched, pulling at the wheel of his chair. If only he could get up, if only he could get into action. Abigail glanced at him and recognised the

113

signs of irritation and frustration accompanying the annoyance at his disability.

She stepped to him and placed a comforting hand on her husband's shoulder.

'Mike, get all the men out there as quickly as possible,' went on Frank. 'If you can pick up the rustlers' trail soon you might nip this in the bud; fail – they'll try again.'

'Right,' said Mike. He turned, swung into the saddle and rode to the stables for a fresh horse.

Frank's lips tightened into a thin line as he watched his foreman go. Abbe felt his shoulders stiffen and she could feel the tension run through him. Suddenly he smashed his fist hard on to the arm of his wheelchair.

'I should be riding with them,' he cried. 'What's the use of a boss who can't be with his men. I should be helping to hunt the rustlers.'

Abigail's grip tightened on Frank's shoulder. 'Mike will see to things,' comforted Abbe.

'Yes, Mike will, but it should be me! Damn these legs, why won't they walk?' Frank's voice rose.

Abbe saw this as an opportunity, but dare she risk it? Would failure upset Frank and undo much of the progress which had been made. Abigail knew she only had a second in which to make the decision otherwise the moment would be gone.

She moved quickly in front of Frank, her eyes brightening with enthusiasm and excitement trying to pass these feelings on to Frank.

'Yes, you should be out there with your men and you could be. It's not your legs; they are all right; it's just you! Come on, Frank, get out of that chair, you can walk!'

Frank stared in amazement at his wife. What was wrong with her? She knew very well he couldn't walk. What had put this crazy idea into her head? Telling him to get up and walk. His brain pounded as Abigail's words went on beating into his brain.

'Come on, Frank, you can walk. Try. Try. You'll never know unless you do.'

Frank was still staring at her. Hadn't he heard? Was she making no impression? Desperately she went on, trying hard to keep out the pleading and maintain only enthusiasm. 'Look at your men,' she went on, hearing the activity behind her as Mike called to the Rocking Chair cowboys and they hurried to ride. 'You could be with them. Frank! You can walk.'

Frank tore his eyes away from his wife and

saw his men running to the stables or to the hitching rails near the bunkhouse for their horses. Mike was there, shouting and cajoling them to be quick.

Then he heard another voice as Matt, grasping his daughter's idea, joined her in telling Frank to try. Frank looked from one to the other. They both seemed so sure he could walk. Why should they be? He'd have to show them they were wrong. Their voices went on; their faces appeared to be willing him to walk. Maybe they could be right. Frank's brain pounded louder and louder with the conflict. He saw the Rocking Chair men mounting their horses. He should be with them. 'You can walk!' 'Try, try!' The riders were milling round waiting for Mike to climb on to his fresh horse and lead them. Frank stared. He should be leading them. He must climb into the saddle. 'Walk. Try.'

Sweat broke out on Frank's forehead as the conflict battered his mind. Suddenly he grasped at the table beside him and started to pull himself up from the seat.

Abigail felt her whole body tighten as she felt for Frank, willing him to pull himself upright. She wanted to go to help him, but resisted the tugging temptation, knowing that to help her husband at this stage would be fatal.

Slowly Frank's body came from the chair. He glanced at the riders. Mike was swinging into the saddle. In a moment they would be gone. He must hurry. Frank increased his effort. His knuckles showed white as he pulled harder at the almost dead-weight which was his body. Then suddenly he was upright, leaning on the table gasping for the breath he had lost in the effort. Mike was shouting his last minute instructions. Frank hadn't a moment to lose. He glanced swiftly at Abigail and Matt.

Delight, at his success so far, mingled with suspense as they eagerly awaited his next move.

'Well done, Frank. Now you can walk.' Abigail encouraged him, hoping and praying that his achievement would continue.

'Sure you can, Frank,' encouraged Matt.

Frank straightened. His legs wouldn't move. He told them to but they would not respond. They seemed as if they weren't part of him. Hurry. They must move. He must get to a horse. His face lined with the effort. Struggle creased his rugged face. Move, move! But nothing happened.

Abigail's heart cried out at her husband's

efforts. Her eyes stared at his legs, willing them to respond to Frank's mind but they remained still. Within himself Matt was pushing Frank's legs. They had to move, they just had to.

Suddenly the pound of horses' hooves broke their concentration. Frank looked up, his mind distracted from its focus on his legs. The Rocking Chair riders were leaving. He was too late! He stared weakly at the dust rising behind the horses as their hoof-beats faded with the distance.

Abigail saw the look and knew they had failed. Tears welled to her eyes, her breath choked in her throat but she fought the desire to give way and cry. Her whole body felt weak as the tenseness drained out of it. She stared at Frank hoping his reaction would not upset the progress which they had made over the past few weeks. She knew a weakening on her part would precipitate despondency in Frank. Without doubt he would feel it, but it must not be allowed to take over. It must not undo the good which had been done. There would be another time, another day when she would be able to seize the moment to get Frank to walk and when that moment came he must be stronger in mind than he was now. She must not show a weakness no matter how she felt.

Frank's strong frame sank slowly into the wheelchair showing the utter helplessness he felt. Silence slowly enveloped the small group on the wooden veranda as the thrum of the hooves on the grassland faded into the distance.

The suddenness with which Frank's fist crashed on to the table startled Abigail even though she was prepared for any reaction.

'Why? Why? Why?' he yelled. His eyes closed, his lips lined grimly and his hands whitened as he clenched them tighter. His head sank forward towards his hands as they continued to beat quietly against the table.

Abbe glanced at her father and rushed to her husband. She placed firm but sympathetic hands on his shoulders and gently pulled him back in the chair.

'Why, Abbe, why did this happen?' he asked. The pleading look in her husband's eyes wanting an answer tore at Abbe's heart. She wished she could provide an answer.

'I don't know, Frank, I don't know. I only wish I did then maybe we'd know who did it.'

'I guess we'll never know,' said Frank shrugging his shoulders. 'And I'm left helpless wondering who and why.'

Abigail wondered whether she should mention Carl Petersen's unusual activity at the party but she decided against doing so, thinking it would only upset Frank all the more, and Petersen's actions could be perfectly innocent.

Frank slammed the table with his fist. 'It is useless, I'll never walk again. You two had better get that idea out of your mind.'

'Of course you will, darling,' put in Abigail quickly as she saw despair crossing Frank's face. 'You're improving every time and I reckon if you try it every day you'll surprise yourself with the progress.'

'Abbe, you saw me today, saw me helpless when I should have been riding with my men. Did I look as though I could walk? No, of course I didn't and you know it.'

'That's not true,' protested Abbe. 'I don't know if you'll walk again, but I do know you have every chance of doing so, but a lot depends on you.'

Frank smiled wanly. 'If I couldn't do it today I never will.'

His voice filled with resignation to what he thought was inevitable. Abbe did not continue to argue. Although she did not like the attitude of resignation, she felt she had won something; Frank had not gone to pieces as he would have done at one stage of his disability. He was mentally stronger now and Abigail saw a good sign in that. She knew it would be a hard fight, demanding all her patience and tact but as she watched Frank now she knew that this new found strength could be her ally.

She leaned forward and kissed him and whispered, 'You'll be all right, darling, you'll see.'

Frank smiled but made no comment.

'Rider coming,' Matt's brief words brought Frank and Abbe back to the moment and to the fact that Matt was still there, something which had slipped from their immediacy with their intentness on their problem.

'Who is it?' asked Abbe, shielding her eyes against the glare. 'Can you make him out, Frank?' she added to divert her husband's mind from the disappointment and upset.

'I'd say it was Carl Petersen from that sit of a horse.'

Frank proved to be correct and the three people on the veranda watched him approach in silence, each with their own thoughts about the rider.

Carl's face was serious when he pulled to a halt. He did not dismount.

'Can't stay,' he yelled, 'but figured it right to warn you there are rustlers around. I've lost nearly a hundred head!'

FIVE

As Carl told his story of the rustlings, Matt eyed him carefully. He had a natural suspicion of the boss of the Flying Diamond but this story sounded genuine enough; there was no reason for Carl to come to the Rocking Chair with a warning about rustlers unless it was true, besides it tied in with their own misfortune. Maybe he had been wrong about Carl, not many disliked him, but few would say they were on friendly terms with him. Most knew him for what he was and so tolerant friendships were usual. Few had the deep suspicion which Matt had and, if he analysed that feeling, he would have to admit the only grounds he had for his suspicions were that he knew Carl had expected to marry Abigail, the man's ambitions, and a hunch.

Matt's thoughts were broken as he turned his attention to the conversation.

'I've sent all my men out hoping to get on the rustlers' trail,' explained Frank. 'The sooner this thing is cut short the better.'

'My men are out too,' said Carl. 'I came over here and one man's gone to inform the sheriff.'

'Good,' said Frank. 'Wish I could ride with you.'

'Sorry you can't,' agreed Carl. 'I'm heading for the north range to see if anybody's turned up.'

Carl raised his hand in salute and his eyes met Abbe's as he turned his horse. He put it into a gallop and was soon out of sight.

'Some big operators must have moved in,' observed Frank.

Strength was added to this opinion, when, around noon, Bob Scammon and his son Hank rode in to inform them that the Hash Knife had also lost cattle.

All efforts to track down the rustlers during the next few days failed. Their trails were lost in the hill country to the north. The sheriff was puzzled and annoyed that he was having no more success tracking down the rustlers as he was in tracing Frank's would-be assassin. Everything seemed to go cold on him.

A fortnight later the three ranches were hit again by the rustlers and the raids became more frequent as success after success apparently lent encouragement to the rustlers.

Whatever precautions the ranchers took were of no avail. They could not protect all their cattle adequately and the rustlers took advantage of this, striking at the points of weakest protection and switching their attacks to different areas of the range.

The continuance of the raids were disturbing to the ranchers especially to those with smaller spreads who had decided to keep their steers until the following year hoping for a rise in prices. If the rustlings continued to succeed, the loss of cattle, with its accompanying loss of revenue, could force them into a precarious position.

It was during this uneasy time that Nancy, who loved riding, decided that her pleasure might be turned to some use if she visited some of the less frequented trails in the hill country.

The summer sun moved into the fall and still it blazed from a clear blue sky. Distant horizons shimmered under a bluish haze which hung over the windless countryside. Old experienced hands predicted no good could come of the continuance of such prolonged weather conditions as the year moved into October.

It was on one such perfect day that Nancy, her thoughts on Bob and her good fortune in having married him, headed deep into the hills for a small secluded valley which had special memories for her and Bob.

She turned off the trail and rose across a broad hillside for a mile. She threaded her way through some scattered trees close to the hill-top, breasted the rise and rose steadily across a flat stretch of land which narrowed as hills rose on either side. Nancy's thoughts were on the day shortly after her arrival at the Hash Knife when Bob brought her across the same countryside and showed her one of the most beautiful views she had ever seen. The hills curved to meet, seemingly blocking the way ahead but Nancy knew of the slight decline in the hill on the west side before it rose and swept round to the east. This drop allowed the rider to cross the hill and as Nancy breasted the rise she halted her horse so that she could enjoy the view and savour happy memories.

Below her a valley, stretching away to the north-east, was hemmed in by hills. A small stream twisted and turned between tree-lined banks. The grass was good grazing but the smallness of the valley made it impracticable for big herds to graze it.

As she stopped, Nancy took in the view with one sweeping glance and was surprised to see some cattle grazing a short distance along the valley, but being on Flying Diamond range and not knowing Carl Petersen's ranch policies she thought no more about it.

She sat for a few minutes enjoying the view then slowly put her horse down the slope into the valley. Nancy followed the stream, living past moments. She had never really tasted happiness until she became Bob Scammon's second wife and she would be ever grateful to him for what he had given her and to his son Hank for accepting her. They had come to be one, close, loving family and sometimes Nancy thought life had been too good to her during the past years. She had found friendship among Bob's friends and she was especially grateful for the friendship of Abigail. How she wished she could do more for her in her present trying time.

She was so wrapped up in her thoughts that she did not realise she had got so close to the cattle. Automatically she halted her horse. Something unusual had penetrated her preoccupied mind. For a moment she could not understand what it was. She glanced round, her attention alerted. Then she saw it again – the Hash Knife brand.

The rustled cattle! Startled by her discovery, Nancy tapped her horse with her heels and sent it forward at a walking pace. She moved among the steers and then she found one of the things she was looking for – the Rocking Chair brand. Nancy quickened her pace but even after another ten minutes searching she did not see one steer bearing the brand of the Flying Diamond!

Nancy was puzzled. Rustlers would not bother to segregate the cattle; brands meant nothing to them. Why no steers with the Flying Diamond brand? She was on Flying Diamond range! The implications of what she was thinking startled her. Had the Flying Diamond cattle been run back among the herds from which they had been rustled? It seemed the only explanation to account for the absence of Petersen's cattle from the valley. If that was so then Carl Petersen must be behind the rustlings! Nancy's thoughts raced. Why should Carl want to rustle Hash Knife and Rocking Chair steers? He was well off, there was no need – then Nancy recalled talk of Carl's ambitions to have a cattle empire and remembered his approaches to Bob to buy the Hash Knife. Maybe he was trying to force a sale. Both ranches had held their cattle hoping for better prices next year. If they lost those cattle things could be awkward.

Nancy wheeled her horse and put it into a gallop, anxious to get back to Bob and tell him what she had found. Steers scattered and bellowed as the horse thundered past. She put the animal at the slope and a few minutes later she crossed the top of the rise, only to instinctively check the horse when she saw Carl Petersen a few yards to her left. Almost in the same moment as she pulled on the reins she urged the animal on. The horse responded and its hooves thrummed the earth in gallop.

Petersen was startled by the sudden appearance of Nancy, but his reactions were swift and deadly. He knew immediately from the look on Nancy's face and from her attempt to evade him that she had seen the cattle and guessed something of the truth. He hauled his horse round, the animal plunged forward and, skilfully handled by Petersen, was alongside Nancy almost before she realised it. Hooves flayed at the earth as the animals pounded alongside each other. Petersen held his horse close to Nancy's until heaving flesh was almost touching heaving flesh.

Even as she tried to turn away Petersen

leaned sideways and grasped Nancy's reins. She tried to beat him off but her efforts were useless and Petersen tore the reins from her grasp. He hauled both horses to a sliding, dust-stirring halt and before Nancy realised it she was lifted from the saddle and dumped unceremoniously on the ground.

The jolt shook her severely and the breath was driven from her body but the instinct of escape was still there and, though her plight was hopeless, she tried to struggle to her feet. Petersen was already out of his saddle and as Nancy rose he flung her back to the ground. Swiftly he was on his knees beside her, his powerful hands turning her on to her back and then grasping her wrists, holding them tight until it hurt and she knew it was useless to struggle.

'You're in a big hurry, Nancy, eager to get away from me?'

Nancy said nothing. Tears filled her eyes which held contempt for Carl. Her sombrero had fallen from her head and her hair spilled around her mingling with the short grass.

Petersen stared down at her. 'Well?' he asked, 'why did you try to ride away? What did you see down there?'

'Enough.' The word was scarcely above a whisper.

'Then that's too much,' snapped Carl.

'And what do you propose to do about it?' Nancy was regaining some of her composure.

Carl did not answer for a moment. His dark eyes seemed to bore right into Nancy. When she had ridden over the rise he had seen her as a threat to his schemes who must be stopped, now he was seeing her as a woman, and an attractive one at that. Nancy had always made him look twice but now in an antagonistic, physical contact he felt there was more than attractiveness.

He smiled the smile of a man who has found the answer to a problem and an answer which he is certain he is going to like.

'What am I going to do, Nancy? Just this.' He bent down quickly and before she realised what was happening his lips met hers savagely. She attempted to struggle but her head was forced firmly against the hard ground.

When Petersen finally straightened she turned her face fiercely to one side.

'Want your hand to wipe your lips?' laughed Petersen.

To Nancy's surprise he let go of her right hand. Immediately she struck out at his face, clawing her fingers. But Petersen was too quick for her. Anticipating her action he grabbed her wrist firmly in mid-strike.

His face darkened momentarily as he snarled. 'Don't do that again.' Then he laughed loudly. 'You look even more attractive when you're angry, Nancy. And you'd better get used to my kisses.'

'Not with what I know,' lashed Nancy.

'Because you know too much,' replied Carl.

Nancy struggled to free herself as Carl's grip eased but immediately it tightened again.

'I'll let you free after you hear what I have to say,' went on Carl. 'You'll not try anything then. You won't breathe one word of what you've seen or heard Nancy or I'll tell Bob what you really are.'

Nancy started, a surprised look, touched with fright, crossed her face.

Before she could say a word Carl continued. 'I see my point has struck home. I know what your life was before you met Bob Scammon – saloon girl!'

'Beast!' Nancy's lips tightened. The word hissed viciously from them. Her eyes, the tears all gone, flashed wildly with hate and contempt for the man who brought up the past she thought had disappeared forever.

'And he doesn't know does he?' Although he only suspected that Bob did not know, Nancy's reaction confirmed his suspicion.

'If you tell him I'll kill you.'

Carl laughed. 'He won't know if you keep quiet about those cattle and, remember I said you'd get used to my kisses.'

'No!' gasped Nancy as the full meaning of his words struck her.

'Oh yes,' replied Carl smoothly. He released Nancy's hands. 'As and when I please. Don't try and look so shocked, Nancy, another man won't make any difference to you after–'

Carl never finished his sentence. Nancy's right hand came viciously across his cheek as she sat up quickly lending greater force to its sweep. For a moment Carl was taken aback. His eyes smouldered angrily then a smile crossed his face.

'I like my women with a bit of spirit.' He grabbed Nancy by her shoulders, encircling them in a vice-like grip, pulling her hard against him, forcing her head back so that it could not escape his fierce kisses.

When he finally released her Nancy sank back on her elbows gasping for breath. Carl stood up meeting her contemptuous gaze with a firm piercing look.

'Like it or not, Nancy, you'll do it my way or that precious husband of yours will learn the truth about you.'

Dejected, Nancy could see no way out. Whatever happened she did not want to hurt Bob. He had given her a new life without so much as questioning her past. She had been thankful that she had always retained something of her Boston upbringing even after wandering in desperation into the life of a saloon girl when she had moved west after her father had committed suicide, following the failure of a business venture, which left his only daughter penniless. That Boston background was always useful when travelling as she had been doing when she met Bob Scammon in Great Falls. She liked him, was grateful for his proposal and seized the chance to escape a life forced upon her by circumstances. Then she had grown to love and now would do anything to save him from the hurt he would undoubtedly feel if he learned his wife had once been a saloon girl. Nancy had told him only a half truth – that she was Boston born and bred.

She thought about pleading with Carl but, knowing the man behind the suave, charming exterior, she knew it would be useless. She knew she was cornered and there was nothing she could do about it. She was confused, shocked by what had happened, disappointed and annoyed at being caught by Petersen. She needed time to find a way out of her dilemma.

Carl extended his arm to help her up but she refused it and scrambled to her feet without assistance. She started to brush the dust from her frock and straighten her dishevelled clothing as Carl walked to the horses which had come together a short distance away.

Nancy had restored some semblance of order to her appearance by the time he reached her with the horses. He handed her the reins.

'I'll see you the day after tomorrow,' he said. 'You know my father's old ranch house, it still has some furniture in, be there at two.'

'What if I can't get away.'

'You'll get away all right. A good job you like riding, it gives you a good excuse.' Carl swung on to his horse and looked down on her. 'And remember, Nancy, one word about those cattle or fail to meet me and Bob gets to know about you.'

He tapped his horse, sending it into a gallop towards the valley leaving Nancy to stare after the swirl of dust which seemed to be closing over the happiness she had found during the past years with Bob.

The strain on her taut nerves was too much and tears flowed freely as she sank her head against the saddle.

During the succeeding weeks the rustlings continued and the ranchers of the district became more and more perturbed. The sheriff, like them, had been unable to come up with any solution to the problem. The hardest hit were the Rocking Chair and the Hash Knife, and both Frank and Bob were wishing they had decided to trail their cattle north and make the usual sale in spite of the lower prices. To all outward appearances the Flying Diamond also suffered at the hands of the rustlers, and Carl Petersen was one who shouted loudest for something to be done about the rustlers.

Carl insisted that Nancy visit him regularly at the old ranch-house which he made more habitable and comfortable for their meetings. Carl was pleased with the way things were going. The Rocking Chair and the Hash Knife would be his yet and with them he would get Abigail if his schemes worked out. In the meantime if he couldn't have the best he would have the second best. So Carl Petersen slipped into a routine which suited him.

Nancy detested every moment she spent with Carl Petersen. After endeavouring to find a way to solving her problem she resigned herself to having to wait until the other ranchers discovered who the real rustler was. She had thought of killing Petersen but feared the possible outcome resulting in her being named the killer with the revelations which would follow. She had thought of telling Abigail and seeking her advice but she knew what that would be. She could not tell Bob, she loved him too much, she could not break his heart by telling him he had married a saloon girl. Now as she watched him being brought slowly nearer and nearer towards ruin, along with her friends at the Rocking Chair, she hoped something would turn up to solve her problem and save them all.

It was this possibility of ruin which began to prey on Frank's mind. While he knew that everyone was doing their best to hunt down the rustlers Frank felt more and more agitated by the fact that he was confined to his wheelchair, he felt he should be doing more and with this began to come the certainty that if had been fit he would have found the rustlers. He became more and more irritable even with Abbe.

Abbe recognised the signs and did her best to counter them, realising that if the rustlings went on unchecked, the situation would be serious not only to the Rocking Chair as a working, financially sound outfit but also to the progress which had been made with Frank.

On two more occasions she used the rustlings in attempts to get Frank to walk but they were no more successful than the effort on the day when the news of cattle rustling first broke. The mental blockage was still there. There were times when even Abbe despaired of ever succeeding but she realised that she must never give way to those feelings, she must never let Frank see that she ever doubted that he would walk again. She kept telling herself that he would, that one day something would happen to make him, she must wait and watch for that opportunity, that moment in time which if missed may never occur again.

The anxiety caused by the rustlings had crept into the men themselves; they were edgy and at times easily upset. It was during this time that Mike Danvers proved his worth as a foreman keeping a grip on the moods of the men, and so relieving Abigail and Frank of some anxiety.

Bob Scammon could see a serious situation developing at the Hash Knife unless the rustlings could be stopped. Accordingly he made every effort to implement this with the result that he and Hank were more and more occupied, giving Nancy more time to be away from the ranch, a fact which Carl Petersen was not slow to exploit.

The anxiety and worry, coupled with Carl's frequent demands, began to take their effect on Nancy. She lost some of her sparkle and zest for life but she put on a front which neither Bob nor Hank, worried about the ranch, detected. Only Abigail suspected that all was not well with Nancy. She first began to wonder when she found that Nancy was frequently absent from the Hash Knife when she called and that she was not seeing as much of her friend as she used to. On the occasions when they met, Abigail sensed that something was the matter, that something was worrying Nancy, in spite of the outward appearance, but she desisted from asking Nancy in case it was something personal between her and Bob.

Matt Clements still nursed his hunch about Carl Petersen and the shooting of

Frank and his natural suspicion of the man automatically connected him with the rustlings but, as Petersen too was losing cattle, Matt was forced to dismiss that idea. Matt's thoughts were also troubled by the situation developing at the Rocking Chair and it came as no surprise to him when Carl Petersen approached Frank again with an offer for the ranch. Both Matt and Abbe were sitting with Frank on the veranda when Petersen arrived. He was his usual, outwardly smooth and pleasant self and after discussing the rustlings brought up the real subject of his visit.

'I know the situation can't be very good for you,' he said. 'You're losing cattle you could normally have sold. I'm feeling it and I'm much bigger than you. So if you want relieving of all your problems don't forget I'm still willing to buy.'

Frank glanced at Abbe but her expression was non-committal. He looked back at Carl. 'It certainly would take away our worries.' He looked thoughtful for a moment. 'Of course I can't do anything without Abbe's consent, nor she without mine, for that matter, so you'll have to let us talk it over first Carl. You can put your proposition; there's no harm done if we turn it down.'

Carl smiled to himself. This was certainly a milder reception than he had expected to his proposal. At least there was the question of considering the offer whereas before there had been flat refusal.

Abigail was somewhat taken aback by her husband's apparent mild acceptance of Petersen's approach but she made no comment. She knew these last few days had been trying for Frank and she was willing to attribute his attitude to the fact that his spirits had been at a fairly low ebb.

She expected Frank's attitude to harden when he had time to think things over. It came as a surprise therefore when, after Petersen had gone, and they were alone together, Frank was serious about Carl's proposition.

'Look, Abbe, these rustlers are posing a problem. Seems no one can get a line on them. They're smart operators and if they continue we will eventually have to face the fact, unpleasant though it may be, of an awkward situation. As Carl says we will be saved a lot of worries, and the situation isn't helped by me being in this damned wheel-chair.'

'No,' replied Abigail firmly. 'We're not selling.'

'Abbe, be reasonable,' pressed Frank. 'I can't see you having more and more worries—'

'It doesn't matter about me,' cut in Abbe. 'If we lose the Rocking Chair we have lost the one thing you are interested in. If that happens where are we going to be?'

'Carl will give us a good price for it. We'll be comfortably off, open a store or something somewhere if you like.'

'What!' There was a slightly contemptuous note in Abigail's laugh. 'You, me, open space lovers cooped up in a store, in something completely foreign to our nature, we'd go mad.'

'Cooped up!' Frank's voice was hard. 'What do you think I am now? Yes, I'm stuck here, you can ride, you can feel the wind, feel the power of an animal under you. How do you think I've felt watching you ride away leaving me here?'

'You encouraged me to go,' Abbe stormed back. 'I was prepared to give that up to stay behind with you so you wouldn't feel that way, but you told me not to. And I thought you were man enough to override those feelings!'

All thoughts of the discussion which had started this had gone and their own personalities and feelings had taken precedent.

'If you were man enough you'd have got out of that wheelchair long ago.' Abigail's words lashed into her husband. 'You wouldn't have remained helpless–'

'There you go again,' cut in Frank harshly, 'saying that I can walk. Can't you get it into your head that I can't and never will. It's me sitting here not you. I know what I can do.' Frank's voice rose shrilly. 'I wish you could just experience it, then you would know I won't walk again, ever! And now you'll tie me to this ranch so I can suffer every time you climb on a horse, every time those cowhands saddle up. All right, all right, if that's what you want for me then keep the ranch!'

Tears welled in Abigail's eyes as Frank's words bit deep into her heart. Suddenly they flowed and Abbe burst from the room. She ran to the bedroom and sank on to the bed her body racked with sobs, her mind tortured by the words which had been flung between them. Within twenty minutes the crying had almost stopped and the confused mind had sorted some things out, only to be left wondering about others. Had she been adopting the wrong attitude all along? Things appeared to be going well but was it only a surface appearance, a front put on by

Frank to mollify her? Was the ranch the right place for him?

Abbe was still wrestling with her thoughts when she heard the door open quietly to be followed by the faint swish of wheels across the carpeted floor. She started to turn over but before she could Frank was at the bedside his hand reaching out and firmly touching her shoulder.

Abbe thrilled as the touch of his long strong fingers surged through her body. She twisted, turned quickly and sat upright flinging herself forward into the strong arms which encircled her body lovingly.

'Oh! Frank, Frank, I'm sorry.'

'No, no, darling it was all my fault.' Frank caressed her hair soothingly.

'I shouldn't have said the things I did,' said Abbe.

'Nor should I. Forgive me, please.'

Abbe pushed herself from Frank's shoulder and looked him straight in the eye. 'Of course I forgive you, darling, but you must forgive me too.'

Frank smiled. 'I've already done that sweetheart.' He pulled her gently to him, and their lips met in a long, tender, forgiving kiss.

'Darling, if you want to sell the ranch we will,' whispered Abbe as their lips parted.

'No, no,' replied Frank. 'I was wrong to suggest selling what has always been your home. I was just worried for your future.'

'Something will turn up. The rustlers must be caught.'

'If only I could—'

Frank's words were cut short by Abbe's fingers gently pressing his lips. 'Sh, don't start again, darling. Let's forget what we said about each other.'

Their lips met again.

But there were some things Abigail did not forget. She had forgiven and forgotten what Frank had said about her but she wondered if she was being cruel to him to keep him on the ranch, witnessing an active life of which he was once a part. Would it be better for Frank if they left the Rocking Chair?

These thoughts still occupied her mind when Carl Petersen rode up two days later. Matt had hobbled to a nearby corral to look over some horses but he made his way back to the house when he saw his daughter come out on to the veranda.

'Hello, Abbe, nice to see you,' said Carl smoothly, sweeping his Stetson from his head. 'Frank around?'

'Sorry, Mike's taken him in the buggy to see some cattle on the north range. Guess you wanted to see him about the ranch.'

Carl nodded. 'Sure did, but I reckon after my last visit it's maybe you who needs persuading.' The leather creaked as he swung from the saddle.

'Seems you're going to try and do that.'

Carl grinned. 'It will be pleasant trying.' He was surprised at Abbe's attitude. He had come prepared to keep working on Frank and leaving him to persuade Abbe but now it looked as though it was going to be easier than he thought. Something must have happened to give Abbe a change of heart.

'I'm not saying I'm selling but it's a serious thought.' She indicated a chair and Carl sat down.

Matt was half way to the house when he saw Carl sit down. He figured Carl had come about the ranch and no doubt he was savouring the fact that Frank was absent.

'–and it's a generous proposition, Carl.' Matt frowned as he caught the end of Abigail's conversation.

'Well, we've always been good friends, Abbe. The offer will stand open for another week.'

'We'll certainly think seriously about it, Carl.'

'You won't!' stormed Matt cutting into the

conversation as he reached the veranda steps. 'What's gotten into you Abbe? Where's the Clements's spunk that got this ranch where it is today? Good grief, lass, if I'd given in over a bit of trouble what do you think would have happened to you and me. You're letting a few rustlers upset you.'

'But, Dad, things are not so good and–'

'Not so good! You'd let a little trouble like this upset your whole future. I said when I handed over this ranch to you I wouldn't interfere but I must if you're thinking of giving it to Petersen.'

'See here, Matt,' cut in Petersen angrily. 'I'm merely enquiring, putting a proposition, I'm not bringing any pressure to bear.'

'I wonder,' rapped Matt quickly. Although he could not be certain he thought that for one moment he detected a startled look in Petersen's eyes, but then it was gone and Matt could not be sure. He turned back to Abbe continuing to speak quickly so she could not pick him up on his veiled accusation. 'It's a mighty good job I split the ranch fifty-fifty; a couple of days ago it was Frank who was weakening and now it's you. What's gotten into the pair of you?' He swung round on Petersen. 'They won't be selling and you can take that as final.'

'I don't think you have any say in the matter,' returned Carl coldly. 'I believe the ranch belongs to Abigail and Frank.'

'Why you young buzzard if I was twenty years younger I'd throw you off the Rocking Chair with my own hands.'

'Dad, please,' protested Abigail trying to calm her father down.'

'No, Abbe, I won't be calmed down. You don't sell the ranch to him.' He glared at Petersen. 'And don't you come round here trying to buy.'

'As I said before I don't think it has anything to do with you.' Petersen returned Matt's gaze.

Abigail pushed herself from her chair. She realised things had gone far enough. 'Please, Carl, I'd be grateful if you'd go.' Carl hesitated. 'Well talk about it again.'

'You won't,' rapped Matt.

Carl's lips tightened, his eyes narrowed angrily, Abbe was frightened, she could sense violence between the two men as old and as lame as Matt was.

She laid a hand on Carl's arm. 'Please go, Carl. Please.'

He tore his gaze from Matt and looked at Abbe, the anger fading fast from his eyes.

'Anything for you, Abbe. I'm sorry this has happened.' He turned, swung past Matt and climbed to his horse.

'I'll bet you are,' muttered Matt as Petersen put his horse into a gallop.

'Really, Dad, was there any need to create that ill-feeling?' scolded Abbe, a look of annoyance on her face.

'Yes, lass, I think there was,' replied Matt firmly. 'Sit down. I think there are things we should talk about.'

'Maybe there are,' muttered Abbe.

Matt sat down facing his daughter but close enough for him to reach out and take hold of her hand. For a moment he gazed lovingly into Abigail's eyes.

'Don't let us fall out, Abbe,' he said quietly. 'I did that because I love you and because I think you love the Rocking Chair and its life too much to give it up. If you left here you'd go into a life completely alien to both of you, you'd never be happy.'

'But, Dad, I've begun to wonder if it is right for Frank to stay among an active life in which he can take no physical part.'

'It's righter than it would be to take him away from it. Here he has an interest in something which has always been his life. I thought you were determined to keep his

149

interest and I thought you were succeeding. Look, if Frank wasn't interested he wouldn't be sitting in a buggy with Mike. It isn't you that's weakening, is it, Abbe?'

'No, Dad, not now. I think I have succeeded in keeping Frank's interest in the Rocking Chair. It has needed a lot of determination on his part as well and it hasn't been easy for him watching active men. He was upset a couple of days ago and it made me wonder if we were right to stay.'

'Of course it's your final decision, not mine. I put in a bit of an act there for Carl, but I was hopping mad with him and I'd be mighty disappointed if you did decide to sell the Rocking Chair just because the going's got a bit rough. I'm sorry if I hurt you with some of the things I said.'

'That's all right, Dad,' smiled Abbe affectionately, 'and thanks for this chat.' She looked at him curiously. 'You seem to have a poor opinion of Carl. He's always been friendly enough.'

'Oh sure he's been friendly when it suited him, and it suited him until you married Frank.'

'You mean he isn't friendly now?' Abigail was a little surprised by the meaning behind Matt's words.

Matt hesitated, looking at his hands thoughtfully, wondering whether he should add his suspicions to his daughter's worries.

'Dad, if you have anything on your mind I'd rather you told me. I haven't given it much thought because I figure it was caused by the shock of what happened and you have never mentioned it again, but I haven't forgotten your outburst against Carl the night Frank was shot.'

Matt looked at his daughter. Maybe he should have voiced his opinions to her before. 'No, Abbe, that wasn't due to shock. It was a cold matter-of-fact view after I'd had time to try to find some reason for the shooting and Carl was the only person I figured had that reason.'

'But I don't see–' started Abbe.

'Then listen,' interrupted Matt. 'Carl hoped to marry you. You can't deny that. When you married Frank he saw his dream of a cattle empire vanishing.'

'Cattle empire?'

'He'd get the Rocking Chair by marrying you. He's tried to buy the Hash Knife from Bob who wouldn't sell. If he got the Rocking Chair he could disrupt the water supply to force Bob into selling.'

'So when he came back from his trip east

151

he got a shock to find I was marrying Frank,' put in Abbe thoughtfully. 'He arranges to have Frank killed thinking that after a time I'd marry him.'

'That's how I figured it,' went on Matt excitedly. 'And things went wrong when Frank was only crippled. But I've never understood why he didn't make another attempt at the second party.'

'I think I can answer that, Dad,' said Abigail and went on to relate how she had followed Carl. 'When we were dancing he quizzed me about the sheriff, he'd noticed his absence.'

'Why didn't you tell someone?' asked Matt.

'What could I prove. I had no real reason for following him. I lost him in the darkness so I don't know where he went or what he did.'

'Well it seems likely that he warned the man he had hidden behind the gun. That would explain why there wasn't the attempt to kill Frank as we expected.' Matt rubbed his chin thoughtfully. 'So now Carl might have given up the idea of getting the Rocking Chair through you, and be trying to force a selling position.'

'You mean by these rustlings? But Carl is

losing cattle too.'

'I wonder.'

'What can we do, Dad?'

Matt shook his head. 'I don't know. We're hog-tied. We've no proof, the sheriff has drawn a blank, the rustlers are too smart to get caught. We can only wait developments and hope Carl makes a slip. If we confront him he'll deny it – the only thing is it might force his hand.'

'We'll do that as a last resort. In the mean-time we'll hold on to the Rocking Chair – the no sale notices go up.'

'Good girl, we'll beat Carl Petersen yet.'

'Just two things, Dad, don't tell Frank what we've talked about, it might upset him and don't you do anything silly.'

SIX

As Carl Petersen rode away from the Rocking Chair he cursed Matt Clements. If it hadn't been for the old man he reckoned he'd have had the Rocking Chair. There had been a noticeable change in Abigail's attitude to selling the ranch. She had been the stumbling block before but now she had softened. No doubt the rustlings were beginning to have some effect. With both Frank and Abigail seemingly heading for a decision to sell, Carl had figured the ranch was almost his. But that meddling old fool had stuck his nose in.

The thought of Matt's interference angered him again. He kicked his horse into a faster gallop. If he couldn't force a sale any other way he would have to get rid of the old man. But first he would try the Hash Knife. Then with land both sides he might be able to pressurise the Rocking Chair into selling.

When he rode towards the Hash Knife ranch-house, past the stables and bunkhouse he was pleased to see no one about.

Carl had a ready made excuse for his visit in case Bob Scammon was at home but it looked as if he and his men were somewhere on the range.

Carl swung from the saddle, tied his horse to the rail and strode to the veranda. Nancy was startled to see Carl at the door when she answered the knock.

'Hello, Nancy, no one at home I hope,' he grinned, amused by the frightened look on her face.

'I thought I told you never to come here to see me.' Nancy's face showed her annoyance.

'There's no need to worry, Nancy, Bob isn't here,' said Carl striding past her into the house. 'Besides this is a business call.'

'Then it's Bob you want to see.'

'No, it's you. And I may as well mix business with pleasure,' he added grabbing Nancy by the waist as she walked towards the room on the right.

She resisted strongly, pushing at his chest with her arms. 'No, Carl, not here, not now.'

Carl laughed as he released her. 'Frightened of desecrating Bob's home?'

'What did you want to see me about?' said Nancy testily, ignoring Carl's remark.

'I want to buy the Hash Knife.'

Nancy stared at Carl, surprised by his announcement.

'That's nothing to do with me. You'll have to see Bob.'

'It has everything to do with you. I've approached Bob several times but he won't sell. The rustling might be making him think again, weakening his attitude. I'm going to step up the rustlings before bad weather curtails the activities. With that pressure and your persuasion I think he'll sell.'

'I can't persuade him to sell the Hash Knife!' Nancy was astounded at the idea.

'You'll have to Nancy or else Bob gets to know about you.'

'Carl you can't.' Even as she said it Nancy knew Carl could and would. She looked desperately at him. 'I never interfere or say anything about running the ranch, Bob would think it strange if I did now. Besides what could I say.'

'You'll think of something.'

'I can't, Carl, I can't. Please don't ask me to do this,' pleaded Nancy. 'Bob will wonder why I'm interfering, he'll find out about us and then about me.' Tears came to Nancy's eyes. 'Please, Carl, anything but this.'

Carl stared at her coldly. 'I want the Hash Knife. You'll work something out to tell

Bob. Think it over, Nancy. Think of the consequences if you don't co-operate. I'll be back for your answer in two days. If you agree then we'll fix the timing to fall in with some more rustling.'

'No, Carl, please, please.'

Petersen ignored the sobs and walked from the room. Nancy stared at the closed door, the sobs heaving her body then she sank on to a chair and the tears flowed freely.

Two days later the stableman on the Rocking Chair led Abigail's horse from the stable. He had saddled it and hitched it to the rail outside the house before two o'clock. Frank accompanied his wife on to the veranda shortly afterwards.

'You'll be all right, darling?' asked Abigail.

'Of course I will. I've plenty to do going into the accounts. I'm hoping the rustlings haven't affected us as much as we think. Mike will be bringing in the reports on the herds shortly, then we'll get down to work. You enjoy yourself; I'm sure Nancy will be glad to see you.'

Abigail kissed her husband good-bye. There was nothing but admiration in his eyes as he watched her ride out of sight before turning his chair and propelling himself back into the house.

Abigail kept to a steady pace enjoying the ride to the river, crossing it at the ford and following its tree-lined banks for about two miles before cutting across the rolling grasslands in the direction of the Hash Knife. As she topped one rise she saw a group of cowboys a considerable distance away and guessed she would find only Nancy at home when she arrived at the Hash Knife.

It came as a surprise therefore when, as she rounded the side of a hill which overlooked the ranch house half a mile away, she saw a man hurry from the house. Abigail halted her horse and watched him swing quickly into the saddle and leave the house at a fast gallop. She frowned when she recognised Carl Petersen's familiar figure as he rode a hundred yards beyond the house before turning in the direction of Lewistown.

Once he had dropped out of sight over a rise Abigail rode quickly to the house. The ranch buildings were deserted and no one was working in the corrals.

The house was very quiet when she went in through the front door which was wide open. She paused inside, then, thinking she heard a sound beyond the closed door on the right, she crossed the hall, to stop at the door and listen. There was no mistaking the sound of crying. Abigail hesitated no longer. She flung open the door and hurried into the room.

Startled by the suddenness of the intrusion, Nancy twisted round on the sofa on which she had been lying, the cushions muffling the sounds of her crying.

'Nancy! What's the matter?' Abigail rushed across the room and dropped on her knees beside her friend, shocked by Nancy's tears streaming from red-shot eyes.

Although the immediate reaction on seeing Abigail was one of shock at being discovered in this situation and of fright that her secret might now come out, the presence of her friend close beside her seemed to bring a comfort she needed at this moment. Nancy flung her arms round Abigail. 'Oh, Abbe, Abbe,' she sobbed and wept unashamedly.

Questions poured on to Abigail's lips but she held them all back waiting until Nancy had cried some relief into herself.

As the weeping grew less Abigail put her questions. 'What's the matter, Nancy?'

'It's nothing, Abbe, really. I'm sorry I'm like this.' The words were interspersed with sobs.

Abigail pushed Nancy gently from her

shoulder until she could look into Nancy's eyes.

'Now, come on, Nancy. I've never seen you like this before. Something big is worrying you. Remember I'm your friend. I want to help if I can.' Abigail's voice was soft and gentle. 'Here dry those tears and tell me all about it.' She offered a handkerchief to Nancy who took it and wiped her eyes and face.

'I'm sorry, Abbe.'

'There's nothing to be sorry about. A good cry does us all good sometimes.' Abbe went on quickly wanting to be of some help to her friend. 'Now, will you share your troubles? Maybe I can help.'

'I don't think you can, Abbe. I've got myself in a terrible mess. Only I can sort it out.'

'Let me be the judge of that, if you will.' Abbe decided to come straight to the point which had been troubling her. 'I saw Carl Petersen leaving here. Does it concern him?'

Nancy looked startled and Abbe knew she had hit on the cause of the trouble. 'You saw him!'

'Yes.' Abbe's thoughts were racing. Maybe this accounted for Nancy's absence from home. She had been secretly meeting Carl Petersen. Abbe was taken aback. Bob and

Nancy had seemed so happy. In her whirlpool of thoughts she could only see one reason for the association, the attraction of a younger man.

'Don't look so shocked, Abbe. It's not what you think.'

'What can I think unless you tell me.'

Nancy hesitated. 'All right,' she whispered, 'I'll tell you.'

Abigail listened without comment while Nancy told her story.

'Oh, Nancy, why didn't you go straight to Bob when you saw those cattle? I'm sure he'd have understood.'

'I couldn't, Abbe, I couldn't. It would have hurt him so much and I love him too deeply to hurt him. Don't tell me to go to him now, I couldn't.'

'All right,' said Abigail soothingly, her mind racing with the new facts and linking them in with what her father had suspected. 'Let's not look at what should have been done but at what we are going to do. Do you know when Carl's going to rustle cattle?'

'No.'

'So we can't plan to catch him red-handed.'

'No.'

'Do you know what he does with the cattle afterwards?'

'No. Apparently they are not always taken to the same place. It was sheer chance I came across them. I wish I never had!'

'You've agreed to try to persuade Bob to sell the Hash Knife?'

'Yes, just now, but I haven't to exert any pressure until Carl has rustled some more cattle.'

'I don't think that will be very long, Nancy,' pointed out Abbe. 'Every day's delay is running the risk of the weather breaking and that will put an end to his rustling until next spring.'

'I've been hoping and praying for winter to start,' said Nancy, 'and instead look at the weather, glorious. What are we going to do, Abbe, what are we going to do?'

Abigail shook her head. 'I don't know, Nancy, I don't know at this moment, but I'll think of something.' Abigail tried to sound reassuring, but she could see no solution apart from telling Bob the whole truth.

She saw she had succeeded for she noticed the relief in Nancy's eyes and heard it in the tone of her voice as she expressed her gratitude.

'Thank you Abbe. I will always be in your debt. I feel a lot better now someone knows. I didn't think I would when we started talking; I thought I would only feel ashamed.'

'You have nothing to be ashamed about. What you did you did out of love for Bob. If ever he knows I'm sure he'll respect you for the sacrifice you made.'

Alarm showed in Nancy's face. 'He must never know, Abbe! Whatever you do Bob must never know.'

Leaving a calmer and reassured Nancy, Abigail rode at a steady pace back to the Rocking Chair. She turned the problem over and over in her mind. Whatever solution she found there always loomed the fact that Carl would talk. Abigail was troubled, she did not want to betray her friend and yet she knew if there was no other solution this is what she must do. She could not see the Rocking Chair and the Hash Knife brought to a state of ruin for the sake of a confidence. Abigail was thankful that she had a few days to play with; Carl did not want Nancy to try to persuade Bob to sell until more rustlings had worsened the situation. But by the time she reached the Rocking Chair she had decided that she could not tell Frank and add to his worries but that must tell her father to let him see that there could be some foundation of his theories and also to seek his advice.

Although Matt was full of sympathy for Nancy he insisted that the best solution was for Nancy to tell Bob but Abigail was determined that they should try to find some other way for Nancy's sake.

'She might not have all that much time,' pointed out Matt. 'If I was in Carl's shoes I'd work those rustlings quick. Winter will soon be with us, this prolonged summer must break soon, and I'd want to get the Hash Knife and the Rocking Chair before then so I could make my plans about running such a large spread and be ready when the spring comes. I reckon if we're to find a solution which will protect Nancy then we've got to do it fast.' He paused thoughtfully. 'Short of killing Petersen I can't think of a way which will prevent Petersen talking.'

Matt was right about the rustlings. Both the Rocking Chair and the Hash Knife were hit hard by the rustlers on two occasions during the following week. Petersen was keeping his eye on the weather, the Rocking Chair and the Hash Knife must be his before the winter. He figured that after the severity of the last two raids the time was right to move in on the two ranches. Nancy must be told to persuade Bob to sell and Matt Clements must be eliminated to leave the way clear for him to work on Abigail and Frank whom he felt sure would be prepared to sell.

Carl wore a worried expression when he rode up to the Rocking Chair and sought Frank and Abigail.

'I reckon we must make another all-out effort to get these rustlers. These last two raids have hit me hard and a couple of ranches to the east of town have also been hit. They're getting too confident.'

'I agree it's serious,' said Frank, 'it's made me think twice about staying on here. However I figure winter isn't far away, that'll stop the rustlings and maybe they won't press their luck around here again in spring.'

'I doubt that, Frank. If we don't get at them now their confidence will run high – they'll be back in spring all right.'

'Well what are we going to do about it?'

'I figure we should get organised in a big way. Up to now it's been left to individual ranchers, the sheriff's done his part but I reckon now we should have one big organised search to find them.'

'Maybe it's a good idea,' agreed Frank his enthusiasm rising. 'I only wish I could sit a horse and be with you.'

'That doesn't mean you can't help,' said

Carl. 'You can put your ideas forward and we can work on them.' He turned to Abigail. 'You're quiet, Abbe, what's your opinion?'

Abigail had been listening carefully, hoping for some slip by Carl, hoping that he might give himself away. But he was too smart and Abigail had to admire his coolness in playing a role which was a lie. At the same time she was wondering what was behind this latest move or was it just one more step in keeping up a front, after these latest raids. 'Well, we've got to keep trying. We may as well go along with you.'

'Good,' smiled Carl, 'I'll call a meeting of all the ranchers who've been hit. We'll hold it in town and we'll have the sheriff there. How about tomorrow afternoon, say three o'clock?'

'Fine,' agreed Frank.

'You'll be able to make it?' asked Carl.

'Sure, I'll come in the buggy,' said Frank. 'How about you Abbe?'

'Yes, I'll come,' she smiled at Frank. 'After all, I've got a half share in this.'

'Good,' Carl showed his pleasure. 'The meeting will be all the more pleasant for your presence.' He stood up. 'Well I guess I'd better be going. I'll get word to everyone else.' He picked up his Stetson and crossed to the door, 'It would be a good idea if Matt could come along. His experience could be a great help.'

'I expect he'll be pleased to come,' said Abbe. 'He'll be sorry he's missed you.' Abbe knew her father would have liked to have confronted Carl but at the same time she was thankful that he had not come face to face with Carl. Now she must find a way quickly to help Nancy.

'Look here, Abbe, I've got to confront Carl Petersen, it's the only way to flush him out into the open. The whole thing is getting bigger than any of us.'

'But Dad, it will ruin Bob's marriage and you wouldn't want that to happen; it's been a good thing for him.'

'I know,' Matt looked perplexed. 'I'd do anything rather than come between Bob and Nancy. Bob's an old friend and Nancy I like very much, but the rustling is getting out of hand. Too many people are involved, there's not just ourselves and our immediate friends to think of, there are ranchers east of town now.'

'I know, Dad, but can't we wait a little longer, I'm sure something will turn up to solve everything,' pleaded Abbe.

'This is just the right time,' said Matt. 'At a meeting like this Petersen will have to give a good explanation and once the affair is brought into the open there will be no point in Nancy keeping quiet any longer, then we've got Petersen on the rustlin' and that might just force his hand about attempting to kill Frank.'

'But it will sacrifice Bob's marriage and Nancy's happiness.'

'If they are big enough they'll weather it.'

'But scars will be left.'

'I'm sorry, Abbe I can't help that.' Matt remained adamant about confronting Petersen.

'Let's get a third opinion, Dad,' suggested Abigail. 'I've kept these things from Frank figuring the worry might retard his recovery but now I–'

'All right, lass. It's only natural for you to want to consult your husband.'

Ten minutes later, when Frank returned to the house, Abigail and Matt told him the whole story of facts and theories. Frank listened carefully as surprise followed surprise and when they had finished he looked thoughtful for a few minutes.

'You sure put a mighty convincing case

against Carl,' he commented. 'It's hard to believe, he's always appeared friendly and yet, if what you say is true, there's nothing to do but confront him with the knowledge you have.'

'But Frank...' Abbe started, thinking of her friend.

'I know what you are going to say, Abbe,' cut in Frank, 'but I see no other way out of the situation.'

After a further hour's discussion Abigail realised she was beaten and had to admit that it seemed the only possible way to put an end to Petersen's activities.

Abbe was worried for Nancy. She spent a restless afternoon, unable to settle down to do anything, her thoughts constantly turning to her friend wondering what the exposure of her past would do to her marriage. Eventually Abigail could contain herself no longer. She felt she had to warn Nancy of what was going to happen. Abbe quickly dressed for the ride and soon had her horse saddled.

She was pleased to find Nancy alone when she reached the Hash Knife. Immediately Abigail entered the house Nancy sensed there was something wrong and that it concerned her.

'What is it, Abbe?' she asked anxiously.

'You aren't going to like this, Nancy,' replied Abigail.

Abigail was obviously embarrassed by what she was going to say and Nancy's mind raced ahead anticipating what was coming. Alarm showed in her eyes as she broke in with, 'You haven't told anyone?'

'I'm sorry, Nancy, I had to tell someone, I needed advice. I knew my father suspected Carl but his ideas were only theories; you confirmed them; I had to tell him. Dad was all for trying to persuade you to tell Bob but I knew you didn't want to so I talked him out of that into waiting to see what happened, so see if we could find any other way round the problem. Now after these recent raids, with more ranchers involved Dad feels there is too much at stake, too many people involved; it isn't fair to them to keep quiet any longer.'

Nancy's right hand clutched at her throat as if trying to suppress the upheaval she felt within herself. 'Oh, Abbe!' The words came as a sob. Her eyes widened, a mixture of disbelief and fright showing in them. 'Please, please, don't let him say anything.' She sank on to the sofa.

Abbe sat down beside her, taking Nancy's

hands in her own. 'Believe me, he doesn't want to hurt you, he loves you and Bob too much for that.'

'Then why?' gasped Nancy.

'This whole thing is bigger than any of us now, bigger than our own personal feelings,' explained Abigail sympathetically. 'Carl has called a meeting of all the ranchers to be held in town, and this gives Dad the chance he wants to confront Carl.'

Nancy felt weak as if she had taken a beating which had left her numb. 'I suppose that's it. This will be the end for me.'

'You don't know, you can't be certain,' pressed Abigail.

Nancy said nothing but shook her head. Abigail spent a few minutes trying to console her friend, then she said goodbye and started across the room. She was halfway to the door when Nancy suddenly realised that her world would soon crash about her.

'Abbe!' she shouted leaping to her feet. Abbe turned round to see Nancy rushing to her. Nancy grabbed Abbe by the arms. There was a pleading wildness in her eyes. 'Abbe. Stop him! Don't let him say anything! Stop him going to that meeting.'

Abigail looked pityingly at Nancy. 'I'll do my best, Nancy.' Her voice was scarcely above a whisper but she hoped it sounded convincing.

Only the clop of the horses' hooves, the swish of the wheels on the ground and creak of leather broke the silence of the still Montana afternoon as Abigail drove Frank and Matt into Lewistown. They were grim-faced, not a word was exchanged as they faced a mission which none of them wanted but knew was inevitable. The betrayal of a friend was hard and each wished there was another way to stop Petersen.

They had covered about two miles when a slight breeze stirred the dust. Abigail shivered. The wind came from the north. Frank frowned and glanced skywards. A few wisps of cloud sped across the blue sky. The three occupants of the buggy turned up the collars of their woollen jackets and inclined their heads against the freshening wind. Matt glanced northwards as they topped a rise. Clouds, torn from the main mass far to the north, scudded quickly overhead like outriders, portents of what was to come. The light was changing quickly and the heat was going from the sun.

Matt grunted. He had seen the approach of winter before. 'Think this meeting's going to be necessary?' he shouted. The words were whipped from his lips by the wind.

Frank shook his head. 'Probably not,' he called. 'When that lot hits us there'll be no more rustling.'

'Want to turn back?' shouted Abigail.

'Better go on,' returned her husband, 'the rustling will start again in spring unless–'

'Unless I denounce Carl now,' Matt finished for him.

The clouds were thickening as the buggy reached Lewistown. The wind rattled shutters, and slammed garden gates as they drove past the neat, white painted houses at the end of Main Street. Only a handful of people were on the wooden sidewalks but the hitching rails outside the saloon were fully occupied by horses.

'Seems most of the others are here already,' observed Frank.

Abigail slowed the horse and drove past the saloon to use the hitching rail outside the bank. She stopped against the rail, jumped down from the buggy and hitched the horse to the wood. She walked round to the side of the buggy and helped her father to the ground.

He nodded his thanks to his daughter. 'I'll be all right now,' he said. 'You go and get someone to help Frank.'

'I'll be back in a minute, darling,' she shouted.

Frank raised his hand and Abigail hurried along the sidewalk in the direction of the saloon. Matt slowly and patiently climbed the two steps on to the sidewalk.

Abigail had almost reached the saloon when the batwings flew open and a cowboy half ran and half stumbled from the saloon. He lost his footing and fell down the steps into the dust of the road. He attempted to get up but fell again. His second attempt was more successful but he staggered and Abigail realised he was drunk. The swinging batwings crashed open again and Abigail stopped in her tracks. A young cowboy waving a Colt in the air swayed two steps to the edge of the sidewalk and stood grinning at the man in the roadway. Suddenly he let out a whoop and fired his gun. The dust spurted near the man's feet. He looked up, annoyance on his face.

'Fool,' he yelled, 'put that gun away.'

The man on the sidewalk laughed loud and replied by firing again. The bullet whined across the street.

'I told you to–' The words slurred from the man in the road and stopped as he tripped and fell in the dust.

Another bullet clipped the ground near his head. The closeness seemed to sober him up for he rolled over and as he came on to his stomach his Colt appeared in his hand. There was a crash and a bullet whined past the man on the sidewalk and shattered the window of the saloon in front of Abbe. Startled and frightened she dropped to the ground. Another bullet splintered the woodwork and bullets flew as the two drunks emptied their guns. When the hammers clicked on empty chambers the two men grinned, staggered forward, flung their arms round each other and, laughing and shouting, weaved a path along the street.

Immediately the shooting stopped pandemonium broke out in the saloon. The batwings burst open and people crowded out. Among the first to appear were the sheriff and Carl Petersen. The sheriff sized up the situation in one glance, drew his Colt and went after the two swaying men, cursing two drunks for being such fools as to draw their guns in their state.

Petersen saw Abigail lying on the sidewalk. Two quick steps took him to her as she tried to get up.

'Are you all right, Abbe?' he asked, his

tone reflected his concern.

'Sure,' replied Abbe as she got to her feet with his help. She was obviously shaken and the colour had gone from her face. She glanced back along the sidewalk. 'Dad!' The cry burst from her lips as she saw the huddled form. She raced towards her father and the sidewalk pounded with Carl close behind her. She flung herself on her knees beside the still form.

'Dad! Dad!' she cried, willing him to speak, but Matt Clements did not move.

One glance told Carl Petersen that Matt was dead. He placed firm hands on Abbe's shoulders. 'Steady, Abbe, steady,' he said.

Tears streamed down her face as she looked in the direction of the buggy. Another shock swept through her when she saw Frank in the roadway struggling to get up out of the dust. She leaped to her feet, brushed away Carl Petersen's hands and was off the sidewalk and beside her husband almost before she realised it.

Thankfully Frank took her arm. 'Frank, are you all right? What happened?' The words pounded from her lips, her eyes wide, fearing the worst in spite of the fact that Frank was alive.

'I'm all right, Abbe. When I saw you fall I

thought that you had been hit. I jumped from the wagon, I don't know how because my legs just wouldn't go when I got to the ground and I fell. Are you all right?' Abbe nodded. 'Matt is he–'

'Dead.' The word was scarcely a whisper.

Frank's strong arms enfolded his wife who sank her head on his chest and wept as he leaned against the wagon for support.

The wind blew cold along the main street of Lewistown.

Two horses pounded along the road and pulled up in a swirl of dust in front of the sheriff's office as Bill Mathews escorted the two drunks towards the building. 'Heard the shots as we rode in, Bill, what happened?' shouted Bob Scammon.

'Couple of drunks letting off steam,' said Bill. 'Two people on the sidewalk when I came out of the saloon after these two. Might be bad.' He glanced in the direction of the crowd outside the saloon. 'Find out, Hank, and let me know.'

'Sure.' Hank turned his horse and rode along the street to the crowd. In a few moments he knew the worst and returned to the sheriff's office where his father and the lawman had just got the two men into the cells.

'Matt Clements is dead,' Hank's face was serious.

'What!' Both men gasped together, shattered by the news about their old friend.

'Bullet got him in the heart,' went on Hank. 'Abbe, what about Abbe?' asked Bob anxiously.

'She's all right. She's with Frank.'

'I must get over there right away, see if I can do anything,' Bob said and hurried from the office.

'What about the other person lying on the sidewalk?' asked the sheriff.

'That was Abbe. She was just going to get someone to help Frank out of the buggy and into the saloon for the meeting when the rumpus started.'

'Sure she's all right?'

'Yes, apart from shock. Doc was just arriving when I came over here.'

The sheriff nodded. He glanced with disgust at the cells beyond the office. 'To think two no-good drunks could kill one of the most respected men around here, a man who helped to make this country what it is. And they'll get away with it. A charge of murder won't stick, it'll be dismissed and a verdict of death by misadventure brought in. I'll have to let them go. I'd like to hang 'em.'

Followed by Hank he stormed out of the office, bent on bringing the town back to normality as soon as possible.

In a cell two men grinned at each other. They had heard every word of the conversation. They knew they had succeeded and were a thousand dollars better off for their act.

Bob Scammon sought out Abigail and Frank as soon as he reached the scene of the killing. There were tears in Bob's eyes as he faced the girl he loved as his own daughter.

'Abbe, what can I say?' His tone faltered.

She reached out and their hands met. 'Don't try, Bob, I know how you must feel.' Their hands gripped in a sympathetic understanding, born of a deep and long friendship. No words were necessary.

'This meeting will be cancelled now, I'll see Petersen,' said Bob a moment later, 'then I'll drive you two home.'

'It isn't necessary, Bob,' started Frank only to be interrupted by his friend.

'But I insist,' Bob didn't want to spell his thoughts out for fear of hurting Frank but he was afraid that if Abbe collapsed with delayed shock things might be awkward for Frank in his condition.

The sheriff had reached the people grouped around the body of Matt Clements. He quickly dispersed the crowd, and the doctor had the body carried to the room behind his house which served such purposes.

Bob sought out Carl Petersen who instantly agreed to a postponement of the meeting and went off to inform the other ranchers of a decision they had expected and immediately agreed to.

'Hank, I'm going to drive Abbe and Frank back to the Rocking Chair. Ride home and tell Nancy what has happened. I'm sure she'll want to come over to see Abbe.'

His son nodded and was soon riding out of Lewistown. Bob helped Frank into the buggy and then, when Abbe was settled beside her husband, took the reins and turned the buggy in the direction of the Rocking Chair.

It was a grim and silent party, still numbed by the shock of the tragedy, who drove the trail back to the Rocking Chair. They hardly noticed the bumps and sway of the buggy and hardly felt the chill which had crept into the north wind.

Nancy came to the Rocking Chair at a fast gallop. The news which Hank had brought sent an icy grip of fear at her heart but she lost no time in getting ready.

'Where's Abbe?' she asked as she entered the room where Bob and Frank were sitting. Her eyes told of her sorrow and Frank needed no words to tell him of her feelings.

'She's lying down, Nancy. Please go to her.'

Nancy hurried away without a word and a few moments later entered Abbe's room. Abbe sat up as Nancy came in and sat on the bed beside her.

'Oh! Abbe I'm sorry,' she said. She looked hard at Abigail's tear-stained eyes. 'I didn't want this to happen I really didn't!'

Abigail stared at Nancy. The words still beat on her mind, '–didn't want this to happen.' Abigail's mind whirled. Surely this couldn't have been planned; they were a couple of drunks. Yet Nancy had good cause to want to stop Matt reaching that meeting. Abigail was shocked at the implication she had presented to herself. No, not Nancy, she couldn't, she wouldn't.

'What do you mean?' queried Abigail, her composure recovered.

'I didn't want any killing, I didn't think there would be.'

'Nancy, what are you talking about?' asked Abbe. 'They were couple of drunken cow-

boys who went a bit wild and unfortunately–'
her voice faltered. Nancy stared at her. The
surprise showed on her face. 'Didn't you
know?'

'No. When Hank came home he told me
your father had been killed. I didn't wait to
hear any more; I came over here as quickly
as I could.'

'And you thought–' prompted Abbe.

'That Carl Petersen had–'

'No, they were drunks. It was an accident.'
Abbe paused and stared curiously at Nancy.
'Carl? Why should he want to kill Dad?'

'I don't know but when Hank told me
about the killing, something Carl once said
came to me.'

'What was that?'

'He said he had nearly persuaded you to
sell the Rocking Chair but your father had
arrived and stopped him.'

'That's right, I remember the time,' said
Abigail. 'And you jumped to the conclusion
that Carl–'

'Yes, but it seems I was wrong.'

Abbe nodded. 'Just a coincidence.'

Nancy looked hard at her friend. 'But,
Abbe, your father's death wouldn't have
happened if it hadn't been for me. If I hadn't
wanted to keep my secret from Bob these

rustlings would have been exposed and there would have been no call for a meeting today and your father wouldn't have been in town.'

'Nancy you mustn't blame yourself. You weren't to know what was going to happen. You couldn't foresee two drunks shooting wildly in Lewistown.'

'No, but if–'

'You mustn't think such things. You had a right to keep quiet. You did what you thought best. I could be blamed as well, after all, I kept quiet, and even Dad did. You can't blame yourself, Nancy.'

'But–'

'No buts.' Abigail cut her short. 'Your secret is still safe. Frank was all for Dad speaking up tonight. There's sure to be another meeting but I think Frank might be persuaded–'

'He might be telling Bob now.' Alarm showed on Nancy's face and she stood up quickly.

Abigail grabbed her arm and pulled her back on to the bed. 'He won't,' reassured Abigail. She looked seriously at her friend. 'Nancy,' she said quietly, 'why don't you tell Bob? There's nothing to be gained from deceit.'

'No, Abbe, I couldn't.'

SEVEN

Two days later Matt Clements was buried in the small cemetery outside of Lewistown. It was a big funeral befitting a man well-liked in that part of Montana. Abigail drew strength from Frank who had insisted on being beside her and had had Mike Danvers there to help him. She had kept a brave face but people knew that deep down Abigail was torn apart. She and her father had been so close, so much of their life had been lived together, drawn closer by the early loss of a wife and mother.

In the memory of her father Abigail drew an added strength; she must not let him down. He was a man who had followed his own conscience and had had the courage of his convictions and she knew he would want her to do the same at this difficult time. She needed Frank, needed his strength to support her in her loss. He was a willing and tender giver but he too needed her. He had voiced his horror, his feeling of utter help-lessness when he saw his wife in danger and could do nothing to protect her. True he had made an effort which had taken him out of the buggy only to find himself freeze and be utterly motionless watching a situation which demanded the action of a virile, active man. Frank needed Abbe's strength to make him see that he had made progress in getting out of the buggy even if he could not remember how he had done it; he needed her strength to prevent any retrograde step in the build-up towards that moment which Abbe felt would come one day.

They both needed each other and in their deep love they found those necessary strengths.

As the buggy topped a rise on its way back to the Rocking Chair Frank called to Mike to stop. He narrowed his eyes against the wind as he looked to the north.

'They're coming again,' he said, indicating the wisps of cloud being driven southwards.

'And that mass to the north is thicker and darker,' observed Mike.

Abigail shivered and pulled her coat more tightly around her. The clouds were thickening. The wind strengthened sending them scudding quickly overhead, driving them southwards, herald of the mass filling the sky behind them.

'Mike!' Frank's voice was sharp, decisive, commanding. 'Hit the trail, quick!'

There was instant obedience in Mike's flick of the reins and shout to the horse. The buggy moved off, gathering speed as the horse got into its stride.

'Faster!' yelled Frank, and Mike called to the horse to obey.

The buggy bumped and swayed and Abbe, startled by the suddenness of the change in pace, grasped tightly to the side to save herself from being thrown out. She glanced anxiously at Frank, who caught the look and smiled reassuringly.

'When we reach the Rocking Chair, Mike, waste no time; get all the men out to the north range. Get as many steers as possible off there into more sheltered places on the northern slopes and get as many as possible near the ranch, use the corrals. If I read the signs right we're in for some severe snow.'

Mike drove fast but skilfully and the Rocking Chair was reached in record time. As soon as they pulled up outside the ranch-house, Mike was off the buggy and reaching up to help Frank on to the veranda where his wheelchair awaited him.

Frank brushed away his proffered hand.

'Get going, Mike! I'll manage with Abbe's help.'

Mike raced for the stables, yelling at the men who were in sight. A few minutes later Frank, sitting in the buggy watched the Rocking Chair cowboys head for the north range at a fast gallop.

Frank turned to Abigail who was standing beside the buggy. 'Sorry to rush you like that, Abbe, but we had to try to do something about those cattle. Now, we'd better see about getting inside it's a bit cold out here.'

In all the excitement Abigail had forgotten the cold until Frank mentioned it. In spite of the fact that the house was sheltering them from the main northern blast the chill which had come into the air made Abigail shiver.

'I can't lift you like Mike does, how're we going to manage?'

'If I jumped down in Lewistown when your father was killed I can get down now,' replied Frank, his voice full of determination. He shuffled across the seat of the buggy and swung his legs until they were dangling over the side. 'Come round here, Abbe,' he said indicating a point near his left side. 'Just in case.' He gripped the side rail

187

with his left hand and the back of the front seat with his right. He shuffled until he was on the edge of the seat and then, taking his weight with his hands, he slid forward and lowered himself to the ground. He managed it without any trouble and, when he was sure he was standing firmly, he grinned at his wife. 'There you are, Abbe, success,' he said proudly. 'No need for Mike to lift me out any more.'

Abigail smiled happily. They seemed to have taken one more step on the road to recovery. Maybe the shooting which had killed her father had served some purpose after all. Frank's mobility had increased, he had found another thing to do for himself, he would feel less dependent on other people.

'Well done, darling. Now we'll get you up the steps.' She put her right arm round his waist while he encircled her shoulders with his left. Abigail knew this was going to be the difficult part.

Frank attempted to move forward but his legs would not move. They would not respond to his prompting. Abigail tried to encourage him with pressure from her arm, but Frank seemed fixed to the spot. Abbe glanced at him anxiously and the lines of determination etched on his face tore at her heart. He deserved success.

'Keep trying, Frank,' she encouraged.

In spite of the cold, sweat broke out on Frank's forehead. Then suddenly he stopped trying and leaned back against the buggy.

'It's no good, Abbe, it's no good.' There was disappointment in his voice. He had been determined to move but it was useless.

'Rest a moment and try again,' said Abbe. She felt Frank had come so near to walking. Two days ago he had jumped from the wagon impelled by the possible danger to his wife, today he had got down from the wagon, forced by the absence of strong help, but there must still be something blocking the final impulse to walk.

'Look, Abbe, with you on one side and the buggy on the other I could drag myself until I could reach the hand rail at the side of the steps.'

Abbe nodded and with a great deal of effort Frank did as he planned. Once he had achieved his first objective, he turned his back on the buggy and, with Abbe's support, leaned forward until he could grasp the handrail. He managed to drag himself the few inches to the foot of the four steps. He grasped Abbe's shoulder. 'Hold tight, darling,' he whispered then, using the rail and Abbe's shoulder, he pushed himself upwards until he was able to shuffle his feet on to the first step. Abbe steeled herself to take the strain as he repeated the manoeuvre. Frank's grasp tightened on her shoulder until it hurt. She almost cried out with the pain at each successive step, but she stifled the cry, knowing that Frank would never make the veranda if he realised he was hurting her. Slowly and painfully they climbed the steps until they were on the veranda and Frank released his grip. He leaned against the corner of the rail breathing heavily from the effort. Abbe hurried to his wheelchair and placed it so that he could twist round and flop on to it.

'Thanks, Abbe,' he gasped.

She wheeled him inside quickly and poured them both a whisky.

It was dark before Mike Danvers came to the ranch-house to report but Frank had seen him, together with some of the Rocking Chair cowboys, driving steers into the three big corrals near the ranchhouse. A few flakes of snow had fallen in the afternoon but the strong winds had driven the clouds southwards and left the skies clear over Montana.

'I reckon you'd better carry on tomorrow, Mike, even though it's clear now,' advised Frank.

Mike agreed and, still having some cattle on the north range, he left early the following morning with five men, having detailed the others to different areas.

The day remained fine with clear skies though the wind still blew cold. As Frank, well wrapped against the chill, was examining some of the cattle brought in from the range, Abigail was tempted to go for a ride as the days left for this pleasure would be few with the coming of winter. Early in the afternoon she headed for the north range interested to see how Mike was getting on. She made contact with the foreman fairly easily and learned that most of the cattle had been moved from the north range. He had split his party and had arranged to meet them on the north ridge in mid-afternoon so that they could pick up strays as they headed back to the ranch.

Abigail decided to accompany Mike and ride back with the men. It was something she used to enjoy but had not done since about three months before her marriage. She looked forward to the ride back as she accompanied Mike to the north ridge.

They both instinctively turned up the collars of their woollen jackets as the full blast of the wind hit them when they moved on to the ridge. They stopped and scanned the ridge but there was no sign of the men. Mike pulled his Stetson down over his forehead for more protection as he looked to the north.

'Don't like the look of that lot,' he shouted.

Abbe shielded her eyes and saw clouds thickening fast to the north. The white, brightened by the sun, was changing colour rapidly to an ominous grey.

Mike searched the ridge again. If a storm was coming he didn't want to be caught in the open, least of all up here. Still there was no sign of the other riders. They turned their backs to the wind but Mike was restless. Every few minutes he turned in the saddle and watched the sky to the north.

Ten minutes later three figures appeared far along the ridge, but already clouds were passing overhead, hastening south, torn from the mass over the far reaches of Montana.

'Let's ride to meet them,' suggested Mike.

They turned their horses along the ridge, closing the distance to the Rocking Chair men. The wind strengthened and they bent their bodies against it. The clouds were thickening fast, the white wisps having fled to the south were replaced by solid looking grey. The blue was being driven from the sky and soon the sun was lost to Montana.

Abigail felt the first stinging wetness on her cheek and, stopping alongside Mike, they both put on their slickers. With waterproof protection covering them like a tent they rode on. They were not a moment too soon. The downpour swept across the landscape with a viciousness induced by the driving wind. Everything was lost to sight. Mike's first instinct was to turn off the ridge and head for the Rocking Chair, he had the responsibility of Abigail but he also had a responsibility to the three men on the ridge. If he turned south now they would not know and might prolong their stay on the ridge looking for him. The rain pounded at them, beating a tattoo on their slickers.

'Mighty glad to see you, Mike,' there was relief in the cowboys' voices when they met a few minutes later.

They were surprised to see Abigail but there was no time to comment.

'Seen the others?' shouted Mike.

'Saw them about half an hour ago about five miles away driving some cattle south,' called back one of the men above the shriek of the wind, which seemed bent on tearing them from the ridge.

'Then they won't get back up here,' yelled Mike. 'Let's ride.

They put their horses down the slope hoping to find some relief below the ridge but there was none. It was as if the wind annoyed at losing a victim made one last effort to take them to destruction.

Suddenly Mike stiffened. The tattoo on his slicker was changing sound and then he felt the sharp sting of ice on his cheek. The temperature plummeted and the rain was gone leaving behind cutting, driving ice. The riders hunched themselves in the saddle trying to envelope themselves in protection against the furious, screaming elements.

Suddenly, dramatically the wind dropped. It was almost weird in its change from viciousness to gentleness as if it couldn't win the destruction of the riders one way it would try another. The ice was gone leaving in its place a swirling whirl of white. The snow came thick and fast blotting out everything with its opaque-whiteness. Soon man and animals were covered and moved through the veil of snow like ghostly riders.

Mike was worried. All landmarks were

obliterated, he was riding by instinct and trust. The snow was thickening and they were a long way from the Rocking Chair. He edged his horse nearer Abigail.

'You are all right?' he called.

'Yes,' replied Abbe. 'I sure hope Frank puts a lantern in the windows. We could easily miss the ranch in this.'

Mike made no comment. Abbe had voiced a thought which had been worrying him and it continued to occupy his mind as they rode steadily on through a world of swirling white. The snow was deepening fast and their pace was slowed accordingly. Mike moved nearer to one of the men who leaned forward in the saddle, the snow piling across his shoulders.

'What do you figure, Clem, have we passed it?'

There was a grunt from the snow-covered figure.

'Another half hour at least.'

Mike said no more until he reckoned that time had passed.

'No sign of it, Clem.'

The cowboy shook off the snow. He seemed more alive to the situation. 'Bear right.'

The riders changed direction following

Clem's lead. Not a word was spoken. Instinctively they had let Clem take charge. Mike new it was their only chance; he was lost and it would be more good luck than skill if he got them safely back to the Rocking Chair. But Mike had every faith in Clem. He had come to the Rocking Chair shortly after Matt Clements had established it and had been there ever since. What he didn't know about this countryside wasn't worth knowing. There were some who said that he knew every blade of grass but even that was obliterated by a white undulating mass. They rode on.

The wind had freshened again and though it wasn't as vicious as it had been it sent the snowflakes swirling, dazzling before them.

Clem swung more to the right. Abe followed instinctively. Then she realised they were riding down a slight incline and swinging round the spur of a hill. She sensed they were near home. Alert now, tense in the saddle she tried to pierce the snow curtain. Five minutes passed, then suddenly 'There, there it is!' Abbe's words screeched out with excitement and relief.

Men were alert in their saddles, eager to see what had attracted Abbe.

'There it is again!' she shouted. 'A light,

ahead to the left.'

No one saw it. It was gone, lost in the thickening veil. The minutes seemed unending. Spirits began to drop again. But those few extra paces lifted the veil. A light shone uninterrupted and buildings, darker masses in the grey-white swirl, loomed large. They were home.

They shouted their praise of Clem and reached the stables thankful to find that all the cowboys were back. Mike rode with Abbe to the house and took both horses back to the stable.

Abigail quickly extracted herself from the slicker, beat the snow from herself and hurried into the house.

'Frank! Frank!' The second call died on her lips as a wheelchair sped from the room revealing a worried and concerned husband.

'Abbe, I wondered what had happened, where you were.' His strong arms enfolded her as she dropped on her knees, sinking her head against his chest, feeling deeply the safety and protection after the clutching icy fingers of the storm. 'Abbe, I was frightened, worried.' Frank held her tightly as if she was some precious thing which he would never let go again. 'It's good to have you back. I thought of you out there alone, lost, in some drift; oh Abbe life would have–' She looked up and reaching stopped the words with a kiss.

'Don't, Frank, don't; forget those thoughts,' Abbe whispered as their lips parted. 'I'm back, I'm safe. I prayed and hoped that you were safely in the house and that you would light the lamps.'

'I felt close to you all the time.'

'And I to you.'

The blizzard raged for four days. It swept through Montana, blew across the Dakotas into Wyoming, Nebraska, Colorado and Kansas. The cattle country was a world of white. The snow eased on the third day and eased altogether on the fourth leaving clear skies. Immediately the cattle world began to take stock of itself. It was inevitable that some cattle would be lost in the severe weather but Frank was pleased he had had the foresight to take precautions. A severe loss on top of the rustling would have spelt ruin. As it was Mike reported very few losses. The shelter provided on the southern slope of the hills had proved valuable and few cattle had strayed from the protection, and not one steer had been lost in the corrals.

Immediately the storm ceased the ranch was all activity as the men laboured through deep snow to take food to cattle unable to find grass. The fine weather continued and was accompanied by a slight thaw but, anticipating that there could be a return of bad weather, Frank kept supplies of fodder moving to the cattle on the range.

Abigail, anxious about Nancy and eager for news of the Hash Knife, left the Rocking Chair on her favourite horse. There was still deep snow about but she was able to pick her way and enjoyed the ride in the exhilarating clear air. But she was not to be the first visitor to the Hash Knife that day.

Nancy was busy in the kitchen. She knew that when the men returned from checking the cattle they would be ravenous. The snow obliterated the sound of an approaching horse and Nancy was startled when the door of the kitchen opened behind her. She swung round, stifling a gasp which came to her lips when she saw Carl Petersen smiling at her from the doorway.

He swept his Stetson from his head. 'I'm sorry if I startled you Nancy,' he said, amused at the annoyance which showed on Nancy's face. 'I thought you'd be pleased to see me with everyone out of the way.' He saw the surprise which showed in Nancy's eyes. He grinned. 'I took the trouble to check that you were alone.'

Nancy's lips hardened. 'You shouldn't be here at all. Someone might return and we wouldn't hear them.'

'They'll be too busy to come back yet, besides we have business to discuss.' He moved to her side and before she realised what was happening his arms encircled her. 'But that can come later.'

Anger clouded Nancy's face as she struggled to push Carl from her.

'Calm down, Nancy,' said Carl. 'This snow has kept us apart and that must be remedied.'

'Carl, please, not here. I told you before, not here!' The words lashed viciously at Carl and he knew it was useless to expect anything of Nancy and as she pushed against him he released her.

Nancy quickly straightened her dress. 'That snow should have stayed for ever.'

Carl grinned as he straddled a chair and leaned forward with his arms across the back. 'Oh, come on Nancy, don't tell me you haven't enjoyed out meetings. After all there's a great deal of difference in age between Bob and me.'

Nancy glared at Carl. 'Don't say anything about Bob,' she hissed and, stung by his insinuation, she struck out at Carl. Before the blow reached his face Nancy felt her wrist in a vice-like grip. She cried out with the pain as Carl jerked her towards him bringing her face close to his.

'Don't try that again,' he hissed, his eyes flashing angrily. 'Maybe we'll leave things as they are when the snow has gone. Now get me a drink and we'll talk business.' He released her wrist which she rubbed as she went to a cupboard.

She poured him a drink and sat down on the opposite side of the table. He sipped the whisky slowly, all the time watching Nancy intently, his eyes seeming to bore into her, while he savoured the power he held over her.

Suddenly he straightened, stretched and then resumed his position.

'Well, Nancy, I reckon you can start putting the pressure on Bob.'

Nancy did not speak and her silence irritated Carl.

'Well?' he snapped.

Still Nancy did not answer.

'Don't tell me you've changed your mind,' he went on. 'Remember what I can do, Nancy, remember what I can do to Bob.' Still Nancy did not speak. Angrily Carl pushed himself to his feet. He stood glaring at Nancy. He wanted his way and he was determined to have it. His voice rose as he went on to remind her of everything. 'Remember I can tell him how he married a saloon-girl; think what that would do to him! I can tell him how his wife stood by and watched his cattle rustled – no, I can tell him how she connived to ruin him – or better still, Nancy, you and I will ruin him, you persuade him to sell and then come to me.' There was a wildness in Carl's eyes as he went on. 'You and I will make a fine pair ruling a cattle empire of the Flying Diamond, Hash Knife and Rocking Chair. We'll hold such sway around here that we'll rule Lewistown as well. How about it, Nancy?'

'Fool!' The word lashed at Carl, piercing his runaway thoughts bringing them to a halt. 'Do you think I'd have any part of that? And don't think you'd get me as far as that by blackmailing me about my past. I'd kill myself first.' Her eyes were cold as she stared at Carl. 'I'll help you get the Hash Knife, I'll do it because I love Bob so much, I'd do anything to save him getting hurt. Beyond that I won't go. As soon as I persuade him to sell, our association ceases.' She saw objections springing to Carl's lips but she stopped them. 'You took advantage of my position to satisfy your desires but once you have the Hash Knife, that finishes, you'll really have no more use for me.'

Nancy knew she held the upper hand for she knew that above all else Carl wanted that cattle empire and to get the Hash Knife was an important step on the way to achieving it. She had only been a useful and pleasurable convenience on the way. Carl Petersen would soon find another woman.

Carl stared at her for a moment. 'All right, you get me the Hash Knife and that will be the end but–'

The door crashed open.

'Hank!' Nancy gasped when she saw Bob's son. Carl swung round. 'How long have you been there?' he snarled.

Hank's eyes were cold as he stared at Petersen. His face grim. 'Long enough,' he hissed. 'You'll not get the Hash Knife and you'll leave Nancy alone.'

Carl grinned at the white-faced boy in the doorway. 'So you want your father to know his wife was a saloon-girl, soiled before he got her.'

'Oh, no, no,' Nancy sobbed.

'He'll only know that I killed the man behind the rustlings.' Hank's gun snaked from his holster as his long supple fingers closed round the butt but he was not quick enough to beat Carl Petersen.

Even as Hank's Colt cleared its leather Carl fired. Hank spun sideways, crashed against the door and hit the ground to lie still.

Nancy screamed and flung herself from the chair beside her stepson.

'Hank! Hank!' she screamed but there was no response and blood flowed from his chest. She turned, wild-eyed on Carl. 'You fool, now everything will come out.'

'Self defence, Nancy,' replied Carl sharply. 'You can testify that Hank drew first.'

'Never! Never!' screamed Nancy. 'I'll never say that no matter what comes out. You're going to pay for this!'

'Nancy!' said Carl sharply. 'You don't know what you are saying.'

'I do! You've gone too far. As far as I'm concerned you drew first and everyone else will know it.' Her voice rose hysterically.

Carl stepped forward and lashed his open hand sharp across her face. Nancy's voice trailed away and tears streamed down her face over the red weal which flamed her cheek.

'Think it over when you're calmer, Nancy.'

His voice pierced like steel, leaving Nancy with no illusions as to what would happen.

Carl Petersen hurried from the house.

Abigail heard the shot while still some distance from her house. She halted her horse staring at the ranch at the bottom of the long slope. There was no sign of life. Abigail was about to send her horse forward when someone hurried out of the house, climbed on a horse and rode off in the opposite direction.

'Carl Petersen,' she whispered and sent her horse forward. It plunged through the snow as Abbe hastened its pace.

Nancy was still kneeling beside Hank, holding his head when Abbe hurried into the house.

'Nancy!' Abbe gasped. 'What's happened? Was it Carl?'

Nancy looked up with undisguised relief that her friend was here. 'Abbe! Thank God! Carl killed him!'

Abbe was beside her friend looking at Hank. 'He's alive!' she said.

Nancy stared unable to believe those words. Hank was so white and so still.

'Nancy! Quick! Cloths, water and scissors.' Abbe's voice was sharp, decisive. It demanded action and Nancy, relieved at the news, obeyed instantly.

In a few minutes Abigail had eased the blood-stained woollen jacket to one side and had cut the shirt around the wound. While Abigail bathed it carefully and staunched the oozing blood, Nancy told her what had happened.

'We can't move him,' said Abbe when she had done all she could, 'so we'll make him comfy here until someone comes.'

Nancy got pillows and blankets and they soon had Hank as comfortable as was possible under the circumstances.

'No,' said Abbe. 'I've got to get the doctor. Will you be all right on your own.'

'Yes,' replied Nancy. 'Please be as quick as possible Hank mustn't die because of me.'

Abigail turned towards the hall but stopped as the front door opened and a snow-covered Bob Scammon strode in. He pulled up short when he saw the blanketed form on the floor.

'What the–?' he gasped looking from his son to Nancy, then to Abbe and back to his wife.

'Oh, Bob!' The shock of seeing her husband brought the realisation that he would have to be told and that her secret would be out and her marriage wrecked.

'Bob, Hank's been shot, he–'

'Shot!' Bob was incredulous. 'What's been happening here?'

'Hank needs a doctor quickly.'

Bob did not waste a moment. He was a man in command of the situation. He swung on his heels and flung open the front door. Snow was falling fast and blew in through the open door as Bob strode on to the veranda.

'Clay! Three of you get over here quick!' he yelled. His voice boomed across the open space to the men who were dismounting at the stable.

Bob turned back into the house tearing off his wet jacket as he did so. He flung it on to a chair and crossed the hall to his wife who was so obviously distressed. He put his strong arms around her and held her tight for a moment. Three men ran into the house. They were surprised by what they saw and questioning eyes looked at Bob.

'Clay, get the doc, quickly!' The cowboy did not wait to hear any more. 'Take Hank upstairs, gently.' Bob instructed the other two men. 'Wait here, Nancy,' he said firmly, wanting to spare his wife any more strain. He glanced at Abbe who nodded her agreement to stay with Nancy.

When Bob had followed his men upstairs Nancy looked pleadingly at Abbe. 'What shall I tell him? What shall I tell him?'

'I think you know the answer, Nancy.'

Nancy nodded weakly. 'I suppose I do,' she sighed. 'Tell him everything.'

'It's the only way,' said Abigail.

When Bob returned Nancy looked at him anxiously. 'Will he be all right?'

'I think so. I've seen men shot up worse than that and live. Hank's a strong boy but he needs the doc.'

'Will Clay get through, the snow it's started again?'

'Clay will get the doc here, don't worry. I sent Hank ahead when I saw the snow clouds piling up, I thought you might be worried about us when it started,' Bob added by way of explanation before putting the question. 'Now what happened here?' He saw Nancy hesitate and glance at Abbe. 'Come on Nancy,' he said softly, 'you never kept anything from me before.'

Nancy looked at her husband. Her face reflected the anguish she was feeling but Bob read at the same time a deep love and a sorrow in her tear filled eyes.

'But I have, Bob, I have.'

Bob frowned. He was puzzled. 'What do

you mean, Nancy?'

'I've lived with a lie ever since I married you.'

'I don't know what you're talking about. What's it got to do with Hank being shot?'

'Carl Petersen was here when Hank got back,' replied Nancy.

'Petersen!' Bob looked astounded. 'Did Petersen do that?'

Nancy nodded. She felt limp and weak as if the very life was being drained from her, but she found words coming out in torrents. Now that she had made the first step the story poured from her lips and she felt relief with every word. She was glad she was telling it and experienced an easing of tension and strain with the confession even though she knew it would be the end of happiness for her.

'Oh, Bob, I'm sorry,' she said with all the feeling she knew when she had finished.

There was silence. Nancy waited for the storm.

Bob stepped forward and put his hand tenderly on his wife's shoulder and looked into Nancy's eyes.

'Nancy, why didn't you come to me when this started? I know you were thinking of me and I admire you for that but you would have saved a lot of trouble – you see, I knew all about you before I married you!' Bob smiled at the astonishment in Nancy's face. 'You don't think I'd marry anyone as quickly as I did without checking on them. Yes I knew you'd been a saloon-girl, but I also found out your true background, but apart from that I loved what I saw there in Great Falls.'

'Bob! Bob!' Nancy flung herself into his arms and wept.

A few moments later Bob pushed her gently away and picked up his jacket from the chair.

'Where are you going?' There was alarm in Nancy's voice and a frightened look in her eyes for she knew the answer to her question even as she put it.

'Carl Petersen has got to be taught a lesson,' said Bob quickly.

'No!' cried Nancy. 'You might get killed!'

Bob smiled. 'I'll be all right. You don't want him spreading stories about you do you?'

'Bob,' Abbe stepped forward. 'Let the law deal with him. We'll get him on a rustling charge.'

'No man enters my house, pesters my wife and shoots my son without me doing something about it, Abbe.' Bob picked up his Stetson and walked out into the swirling snow.

'Stop him! Stop him!' screamed Nancy and ran to the door. She flung it open and ran on to the veranda. 'Bob! Bob!' she yelled at the shadowy figure striding purposefully towards the stables. She felt Abbe's hands take hold of her firmly and lead her back into the house as the figure was lost behind a curtain of snow. Tears were streaming down Nancy's face. 'I don't want to lose him Abbe, I don't.'

'I'll try to stop him,' said Abbe comfortingly. 'You do what you can for Hank. Sit with him in case he regains consciousness before the doc comes.'

Nancy nodded, wiped her eyes and hurried up the stairs.

Abigail put on her jacket and went outside. She brushed the snow quickly from her horse and from the saddle and rode to the stable. She hurried inside to find Bob leading his saddled horse from the stall.

'Bob,' she said, 'for Nancy's sake don't go; let the law handle this.'

Bob's face was serious. 'Abbe, you know what your father would have done in my place.' Abbe nodded. There was no denying

211

that he would have done exactly the same. 'I wonder about your father's death; was it really an accident or was it planned by Petersen? I've got to go Abbe after what he's done to Nancy and Hank, but you know, maybe I'll be doing it for an old friend as well.'

'Bob, please. I'm thinking of Nancy. If anything happens to you–' Abigail stood belligerently in his path.

'That's a risk I'll have to take,' said Bob. 'I've got to go, out of respect to myself; I'd never face Nancy with ease again if I didn't face Carl Petersen now. So don't try to stop me.'

Abbe held her ground as Bob came forward. He stopped in front of her, his large frame towering over her.

'Abbe, please' he said quietly. 'I don't want to hurt the daughter of my old friend.'

Abigail shrugged her shoulders and stepped to one side. She knew he had to go. Bob brushed past her quickly and was gone, lost in the snow which was thickening fast. Abbe stood at the door of the stable gazing after him and then she looked to the house. Nancy! She couldn't let it end here; she must do something for Nancy's sake. She ran to her horse, climbed into the saddle and headed as fast as the snow allowed for the Rocking Chair. She must get someone to Flying Diamond to protect Bob. Abigail urged her horse on and the strong animal answered her call.

The falling snow eased and when Abigail approached the Rocking Chair it had almost stopped. She had left the thick grey mass behind her, with little wind its drift was only slow and as yet had brought little fresh snow to the Rocking Chair range. Although it meant easier riding, Abbe knew it also meant that Rocking Chair cowboys would not have returned. Anxiety gripped her as she approached the buildings and her fears were confirmed when she visited the stable; no one was back!

She looked round desperately, hoping to see some black figure darkening the snow-covered landscape but there was none. She swung into the saddle and rode quickly to the house. Something had to be done and done quickly. Abbe leaped from the horse before it stopped and ran to the house.

'Frank! Frank!' she shouted and ran into the room almost before Frank had started to move his wheelchair towards the frantic call.

'Abbe! What's the matter?' Frank's voice was full of concern when he saw Abbe's dishevelled appearance after her fast ride.

'Frank, Bob's gone after Petersen, he must be stopped!'

'What on earth are you talking about?'

'Petersen's younger, faster. He'll kill Bob!' cried Abbe desperately. 'Where are the men, someone must go.'

'Abbe!' Frank's voice was sharp trying to stop Abigail's incoherent words. 'Tell me what it's all about?'

Abigail blurted out the story quickly. 'Oh! Frank, we've got to save Bob.' She looked desperately at her husband when she finished. 'Frank, if you're going to walk, walk now! Get to the Flying Diamond before it's too late!'

The shock of her words hit Frank. He stared at her in astonishment. 'I can't walk, Abbe!'

'Of course you can!' Abbe's eyes were wide. 'You can walk! You always could!' Her voice rose. 'You have no physical handicap! You–'

'Abbe!' Frank shouted to be heard above Abbe. 'I was shot in the back – remember – paralysed. I can't walk!'

The sharpness in Frank's voice brought Abbe from the edge of hysterics. She looked hard at her husband sitting in his wheelchair. 'You can walk,' she replied obstinately. 'It's just that you haven't tried hard enough, and if you won't try now, when Bob's life is in danger and Nancy's happiness is in jeopardy, you never will.' Her voice was cutting, hurting Frank, 'You'll be stuck in a wheelchair for the rest of your life when you could be leading a normal life.'

Frank thumped the arm of his chair. 'I'm paralysed. Can't you get it into your head, I can't walk!'

'You can!' snapped Abbe. 'If you won't try to help Bob, then I must!'

Abigail swung on her heels and ran from the house.

'Abbe!' Frank yelled and propelled his chair on to the veranda.

Abigail was already in the saddle and turning her horse.

'Abbe!' he shouted again but she took no notice. With his mind battered by his wife's words Frank watched his wife gallop away. His face was grim as he bowed his head and stared at his legs.

'Walk, curse you, walk!' he screamed.

His brain pounded. Abbe was riding into danger. The last time her life had been threatened he had tried to go to her help, he had got out of the buggy but then no further. Now the danger was worse for she would be desperate to save Bob.

Frank turned his chair to face the veranda rail. He grasped them tightly; his lips hardened in a grim line. Tensing his arms, he pulled himself to his feet.

'Now, walk,' he muttered. 'Walk.' Nothing happened. He cursed and then angrily pushed the wheelchair away. 'Now you'll have to walk!' he shouted, but his legs continued to mock him with their uselessness. Sweat broke out on his forehead as he tried desperately to go to save his wife. His mind kept pounding her name, he kept seeing a gunfight she must be riding into and all the time her face kept getting bigger and bigger until he thought his brain would burst.

The first flakes of snow started to fall from the leadened sky as the wind freshened driving the clouds across the Rocking Chair.

Abigail kept her horse to a fast pace. It would be touch and go whether she would get there in time. Bob Scammon could not be too far ahead for he had to cross the Rocking Chair before coming to the Flying Diamond. She felt the bite of the wind as she topped a rise and the snow drove more fiercely. The wind strengthened as if trying to stop her, as if it was an ally of Carl Petersen. Abbe urged her horse faster and the strong animal responded sending the snow flying beneath its hooves.

Abigail had seen no sign of Bob by the time the Flying Diamond loomed black against the falling snow. Her thoughts pounded. Was she too late? Had her effort been in vain? There was no sign of Bob's horse but he would not ride right up to the house, was he already there or did she still have time?

Abbe halted her horse a short distance from the house, slipped from the saddle and tied it to the corral rail. She hurried through the swirling snow but pulled up short when she saw a shadowy form moving steadily along the veranda. There was no mistaking Bob's bulky frame.

'Bob!' Abbe called but her word was swept away by the wind and Bob moved to the door of the house. Abbe started to run but she was too late. Bob stepped into the house.

Panic seized her; her legs didn't seem to be moving, the snow dragged at her feet seeming to hold her back. Any moment she expected to hear a shot but none came. Then she was on the veranda, hurrying towards the front door. She faltered in her step. The silence of the house struck her as unnatural. Where she had expected noise, the crash of a gun, the shouts of men, there was nothing. Snow fell silently. Only the wind moaned its existence. Abbe slowed and as if by compulsion opened the door quietly. She stepped into the hall and looked around. The house was still. Only the tell-tale wetness on the floor indicated the presence of a human being. The marks led to the closed door on the right. She started towards it but pulled up short when she heard a click and a voice beyond it.

'All right, Bob, drop that gun.'

Abbe started. It was Petersen's voice. He must have entered the room by another door. Abbe heard a clatter followed by Petersen again but with some of the tension out of his voice.

'That's better. I've been expecting you Bob. My first inclination on killing Hank was to get the sheriff. It was a case of self-defence, Nancy would have verified that. But I figured you'd come gunning for me – well it gives me the opportunity to get rid of you, self-defence again, and then the Hash Knife will be mine.'

Bob's face was grim. He had walked into a trap. He must play for time to find some way out of it. Bob glared angrily at Petersen.

He felt like leaping at him but the gun held him back.

Petersen laughed. 'You'd like to horsewhip me wouldn't you?'

'It's what you deserve,' stormed Bob. 'Using a woman, blackmail, rustling,' there was contempt in Bob's voice, 'you aren't your father's son, at least he would have fought clean.'

Petersen grinned. 'I'm sorry it had to come to all those things, oh, I'm not sorry about Nancy, that was pleasure.' He saw Bob stiffen and the tension of a coiled spring come into his body. 'Hold it there,' he warned. 'None of it would have happened if my fool foreman hadn't muffed his shot at Abigail's wedding.'

'So it was you,' hissed Bob. 'Matt guessed it was and that's why you had him killed.'

Petersen's grin broadened. 'I didn't know Matt suspected me, seems I did right to get him out of the way. I'd have had the Rocking Chair but for him. Abbe and Frank needed very little more persuasion to sell but that old fool stuck his nose in.'

'So then you switched your attention to the Hash Knife.' Bob wanted to keep him talking.

'Sure if I had one or the other I figured I could force the other to sell. It would have been easier with the Rocking Chair.'

'You'd have interfered with my water supply.'

'Right,' laughed Petersen. 'Well, I still win, it's going to be easy to get the Hash Knife with you out of the way.'

'The Hash Knife won't be vacant.'

Petersen laughed. 'Don't tell me Nancy will run it.'

'There's Hank.'

'He's dead.'

'He's not. You didn't kill him. You'd have to commit murder again.' Bob saw Petersen was shaken by the news. 'So you see Petersen all your efforts have been useless, you—'

'Shut up,' Petersen snapped. His mind was racing. Was Bob bluffing? If he wasn't things could be awkward. A grin crossed his face. 'If you aren't bluffing I figure I can get rid of him easy enough.'

The door burst open. Abbe had heard enough. 'You'll have to get rid of me too!'

Both men were startled by the suddenness of Abigail's appearance. Petersen was thrown off his guard. Bob seized at the half chance. He grabbed for his gun on the floor. Petersen flung his Colt back and before Bob could touch his gun Petersen squeezed the trigger. Noise filled the room and Bob staggered grasping at his shoulder.

'Fool!' Petersen snarled. 'The next one is the end for you. As for you, Abbe, a prowling figure in the snow, a shot, how was I to know it was you. I'd hoped to marry you but you know too much. Maybe Nancy–'

'She won't,' Bob snapped in spite of the pain.

'She certainly won't!' The voice boomed from the open door.

Carl swung round looking as if he had seen a ghost, then he was squeezing the trigger. But the slight hesitation at the shock proved fatal. Even as he fired a bullet took him in the chest and as he collapsed his own crashed harmlessly onto the floorboards.

'Frank!' Abbe was startled at the sight of the snow covered figure standing in the doorway. Then she flung herself forward into his arms ignoring the wetness. She looked up with tears of relief and happiness flowing from her eyes. 'How – who helped – you're walking–'

Frank smiled. 'I couldn't sit there and see my wife ride into danger, which I should be dealing with.' He eased her gently away, holstered his gun and with one arm round her helped Bob to his feet.

'Come on, old friend, let's get home. It's

snowing heavy, but we'll survive the winter and use the Flying Diamond as well as our own spreads next year.'

The publishers hope that this book has given you enjoyable reading. Large Print Books are especially designed to be as easy to see and hold as possible. If you wish a complete list of our books please ask at your local library or write directly to:

Dales Large Print Books
Magna House, Long Preston,
Skipton, North Yorkshire.
BD23 4ND